My Travels with Capts. Lewis and Clark, by George Shannon

a novel by KATE McMULLAN

with art by ADRIENNE YORINKS

JOANNA COTLER BOOKS
HarperTrophy®
An Imprint of HarperCollinsPublishers

My Travels with Capts. Lewis and Clark, by George Shannon
Text copyright © 2004 by Kate McMullan
Illustrations copyright © 2004 by Adrienne Yorinks
Map copyright © 2006 by Jim McMullan

www.harperchildrens.com

Library of Congress Cataloging-in-Publication Data
McMullan, Kate.
    My travels with Capts. Lewis and Clark, by George Shannon / a
novel by Kate McMullan ; with art by Adrienne Yorinks.
        p. cm.
    Summary: A fictional journal recounting the travels—from
Pittsburgh to the Pacific Ocean—of sixteen-year-old George Shannon, the
youngest member of Lewis and Clark's Corps of Discovery.
    ISBN-10: 0-06-008101-5 — ISBN-13: 978-0-06-008101-0
    1. Shannon, George, 1786 or 7–1836—Juvenile fiction. 2. Lewis
and Clark Expedition (1804–1806)—Biography—Juvenile fiction. [1.
Shannon, George, 1786 or 7–1836—Fiction. 2. Lewis and Clark
Expedition (1804–1806)—Fiction. 3. Overland journeys to the Pacific—
Fiction. 4. Diaries—Fiction.] I. Yorinks, Adrienne, ill. II. Title.
PZ7.M47879Ge 2004   2003011754
[Fic]—dc22   CIP
                                                                 AC

Typography by Alicia Mikles
❖
First Harper Trophy edition, 2006

For Dick, Nancy, Jim, Carolyn, Bill, Bob,
Linda, and Ned.
—K.M.

For my husband, Doug.
—A.Y.

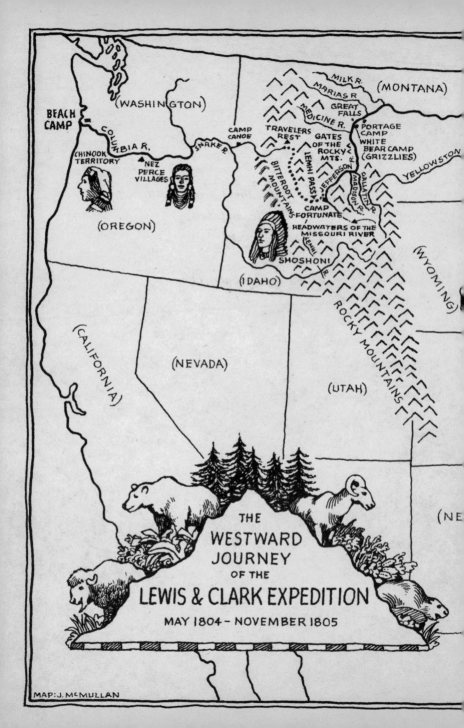

THE
WESTWARD
JOURNEY
OF THE
LEWIS & CLARK EXPEDITION
MAY 1804 – NOVEMBER 1805

MAP: J. McMULLAN

Shannon Farm, Ohio

Dearest George,

We send this journal with our love on your sixteenth birthday.

Thomas, John, James, and David tanned the hide for its cover. Nancy, Lavinia, and Arthur stitched it up. Even little Wilson helped to trim the pages. Didn't they do fine? We miss you, George. We long to look into your clear blue eyes and hear your cheering songs, but we know you are using your time away from us to good purpose, working hard at your studies, and learning all that your uncle has to teach you in the shop. With your pa gone now, we are counting on you, George.

Love,
Ma

"In writing of your days, may you come to know your heart."

If I write of this day, I must say I counted nails, screws, nuts, bolts, brads, hooks, and locks. I thought I was done when Peter, the shop's errand boy, rolled in a fresh keg of nails, and I started counting again.

This evening I plunked myself down at the kitchen table and toted up my inventory. Uncle Liam kept his hawk eye on me. Twice I added wrong and he thumped me on the head. Hard, too.

At last I got the sums added up. Then Uncle said he must see my geography lesson, and I had to confess that somehow the geography book has gone missing.

"You find it, boy," Uncle said, "or I will yank down your breeches and tan your bottom."

"Just you try it, Uncle. I may be scrawny, but I am strong. We'll see who gets tanned!"

Or so I wish I'd said.

July 22, '03

Uncle Liam had just stepped out of the shop this afternoon when a gentleman came in. He said he'd been promised handsaws at $1^1/_2$¢ each, and I sold him all we had at that price. When Uncle came back and learned of the sale, he started screeching how handsaws go for 3¢ apiece, and I'd been cheated. He picked up a hammer, but I ran out of the shop before he could thump my head with *that*.

Snagged my breeches on a nail and tore a hole. I got out the little red "housewife" kit stuffed with needles, threads, and such that Ma gave me when I left home. I had a devil of a time poking the thread into the needle eye, but at last I got her through and stitched up the tear. A neat job, too.

July 23, '03

Uncle Liam saw me stitching. Tonight after supper, he handed me two pairs of holey socks to mend. I am half glad for his socks, as they took Uncle's mind off my lessons.

No sign of the geography book.

How Ma's sister came to marry Uncle Liam, I will never understand.

July 30, '03

Uncle Liam dished out rice and beans for supper. I spied chunks of pork in his bowl, but search as I might, I found none in mine. When I asked why, Uncle said, "You eat like a horse, boy. I can't hardly afford to keep you in beans."

Uncle complains of a toothache.

Aug. 3, '03

Uncle Liam's tooth still nags him. The barber could pull it, but my uncle says he won't spend good money on a bad tooth.

I turned my room upside down, looking for *Geography Made Easy*. No luck.

Aug. 4, '03

Uncle shook me awake in the night. His rotten tooth was paining him bad, and he said I must yank it. I followed him to the kitchen, where he gulped down some whiskey. Then he handed me the pliers, pressed his back to the wall, and opened wide. Uncle's breath stank worse than old Red Dog's back home, and the lantern gave poor light, but at last I found the culprit way in the back of his mouth and got a grip. I pulled. Uncle Liam hollered. We kept this up for a while, but nothing came of it. Next I braced my foot against his gut, and twisted and wrenched that tooth in a most horrible manner, but it would not be yanked. At last Uncle shoved me aside. He staggered off to bed, saying it is a good thing I am not a tooth-puller's apprentice.

For once, I agree with my uncle.

Aug. 5, '03

The barber pulled the tooth. Uncle Liam brought it home. He says he paid so much for this tooth, it would be a shame to toss it out, so he set it on the mantle for a decoration, propped up against the frame holding a lock of hair from Ma's poor dead sister.

***

Peter is fevered. Uncle says I must run to the wharf in his stead to fetch a batch of hinges. At last I am to escape this musty shop!

No sooner had I set foot on the wharf than a hairy black beast lunged at me and knocked me down. I grabbed the monster's throat. I was near to choking the life out of it when a man shouted, "Seaman, off!" The beast leaped from me.

A tall, yellow-haired man in a military jacket put out a hand and hauled me to my feet. He asked if I was hurt. I said I was not but backed away, saying I'd never been up close to a bear.

The man laughed. "This is no bear," he said. "Seaman is a Newfoundland dog, a breed known to be most gentle and intelligent." He added that he was puzzled as he had never known his dog to leap on anyone before.

The man gave me his name then: Captain Meriwether Lewis. His shaggy dog eyed me, very eager. He put me in mind of my old Red Dog, hoping for supper scraps, and I guessed the reason for the attack. From my breast pocket I drew one of the dried beef sticks I've taken to carrying to ease my hunger pangs between meals. I held it out, Seaman took it, and we became fast friends.

Capt. Lewis said, "Young man, would you care to see a great marvel?"

I cared to, and he led the way down the wharf,

4

stopping beside a half-finished boat.

"I designed her myself," the Captain said proudly. "She is 55 feet long. When complete, she will have a cabin at the stern and benches for twenty-two men pulling oars."

I asked where he was bound in such a fine craft, and his eyes lit up.

"If the whiskey-guzzling sluggard of a boatbuilder ever finishes her up," he said, "I will shove off for the Pacific Ocean!"

A thousand questions bubbled up inside my head, but I had no chance to ask them, for the Captain caught sight of this same boatbuilder and charged off to speak with him. Uncle's hinges were waiting, and so I went my way.

Cannot sleep for thinking of Capt. Lewis. I have studied enough geography to know that a ship going to the Pacific Ocean sails around the tip of South America. The Captain must be addle-headed to think of making an ocean voyage in that small boat.

Aug. 11, '03

Peter is still fevered. Today Uncle sent me to the wharf of the boat. As I neared it, Seaman bounded over to greet me. I rubbed the dog's head and listened to Capt. Lewis telling the boatbuilder: "Sir! I must travel down the Ohio River and up the Mississippi River to the mouth of the Missouri River before winter sets in! Yet here I stand on a Pittsburgh wharf, waiting. Waiting! Hire more carpenters, sir! Set longer hours! Do whatever it takes to finish my boat!"

The boatbuilder spat on the dock. He said he'd had enough of being rushed by a high-and-mighty captain. He staggered off, heading for the Grog and Gobble, and his men began packing up their tools. Capt. Lewis pulled a bag of coins from his pocket. Within minutes, the hammering and sanding had started up again.

Only then did Capt. Lewis see me standing there. I said what a wonder that such a small bag could accomplish such a big task. He laughed and asked me to walk with him a spell. He said after trying to talk to the bull-headed boatbuilder, he would welcome a conversation with a bright young man. We left the wharf, heading down a narrow street. Seaman trotted at his master's side. The Captain told me that the dog was so named because he had been born aboard a ship, and that he had bought him from a sailor for $20. Twenty dollars! Why, the Captain could have bought three good horses for that price.

As we walked, I worked up my nerve and finally asked: "Sir, do you believe your boat sturdy enough for a long ocean voyage?"

"I will not sail any ocean," the Captain said. "My men and I will row up the Missouri River to the mountains where it meets the Columbia River, then sail down the Columbia to the Pacific Ocean." He told me that this all-river route across the continent is called the Northwest Passage.

I confessed that in studying the maps in my geography book, I had never seen the place where these two great rivers meet.

The Captain nodded. He said that no one has quite discovered this passage yet, but both he and President Jefferson are sure that it exists.

"I shall find the Northwest Passage," the Captain said. "Then—think of it! Goods can be shipped from one end of our great American continent to the other!"

Capt. Lewis told me that President Jefferson wishes him and his party of soldiers to befriend the Indians as they go and make peace among all tribes. They are to map the western territory, and keep Scientific Notebooks with drawings of all they see, for President Jefferson believes volcanoes may still be spewing fire out west. Woolly mammoths and saber-tooth tigers may yet roam the western plains. Capt. Lewis has even heard it said that the west is home to beavers 7 feet tall!

"The President promises a reward of many acres of western land to all who go along on this western expedition," Capt. Lewis said. "The sooner we shove off, the better."

It was mighty hard to tear myself away from tigers and giant beavers to fetch two dozen barrel hoops.

I found the geography book! I cannot think how it came to be lodged behind my bed. Page 14 shows a drawing of the Missouri River. It winds like a giant snake from St. Louis to the Rocky Mountains. From these mountains to the Pacific Ocean is a wide stretch labeled PARTS UNKNOWN. Oh, what a great adventure Capt. Lewis and his men will have! I wish I might have even one small adventure before I am apprenticed to Uncle and become George Shannon, assistant shopkeeper.

Aug. 13, '03

Peter is recovered. I am doomed to work inside the shop today. And every day from here on out.

Aug. 15, '03

I gave Peter an apple. I said he must rest and regain his health, and that I would go to the wharf for him to fetch the items on his list. He was ever so grateful.

I ran the whole way there. For Capt. Lewis's sake, I tried to hope that the builder had finished his boat, that the Captain and his soldiers were on their way down the Ohio River. But when Seaman came bounding toward me, I felt such a joy that this was not the case that I fed the dog two beefy sticks.

The boat is nearly finished. The workers were setting up poles to hold a canvas roof over the stern. Capt. Lewis calls this craft a keelboat. He showed me its keel, a long beam going all the way down the middle of its flat bottom. The Captain believes it is the finest craft ever built. He was in high spirits and suggested another walk. As we went, he mentioned that, in addition to soldiers, he is looking for a dozen young men to go along on his expedition.

"Young men?" I said.

"Strong, healthy young men," said the Captain. "Unmarried young men of good character. Young men who can bear great bodily fatigue and are entirely at home in the woods." He asked if I knew of any such young men.

Words sprang from my mouth. "I am such a young man, sir! I can bear the most punishing sort of fatigue. I am completely at home in the woods." (So I always felt when chasing our strayed pigs.) "I am strong and healthy as a horse. I have an excellent character and I am not in the least bit married."

Hearing this, the Captain threw his head back and laughed.

"You are far too young and skinny to be part of the crew I have in mind," he said. "You are still a pup, growing into your paws. I know all about growing pups." He gave Seaman a pat. "Pups eat too much. Pups cost too much to feed."

My longing to go was so strong that I could not take his words to heart. I begged him to give this pup a try going down the Ohio.

The Captain shook his head. He was about to turn me down when Seaman barked. He jumped up, resting his paws on my shoulders. Capt. Lewis threw an arm around his dog. He declared that if Seaman wanted a fellow pup on board going down the Ohio, who was he to object? But he warned me again and again: "This is a trial only, and in no way an offer for the Expedition."

I have never met a man with such a high regard for his dog's opinion. I am one lucky pup!

Uncle Liam suffers sour stomach tonight. I think it best not to worry him with my plans.

Aug. 22, '03

Cannot sleep. I write by candlelight. Ma has eight mouths to feed. In this very journal, she wrote, "We are counting on you, George." Counting on me to work for Uncle Liam. Counting on me to send home money for the family. Ma, just this once, please count on Thomas. He is only one year my junior. Or on John. Or James. You have so many sons! If I am picked to go on this great Expedition—think of it, Ma!—how can I turn down such a chance? Oh, Ma, if I go, can you forgive me?

Aug. 30, '03

I wrote to Uncle Liam. I finished up by saying, "I am sorry to disappoint you, Uncle, but I cannot resist this call to Adventure." I will leave a quarter to pay for *Geography Made Easy*, as I am taking it along. By the time Uncle Liam finds my letter, I hope to be on a keelboat going down the Ohio River with Captain

Meriwether Lewis, United States Army.

I will write to Ma from the river.

The carpenters banged the last nail into the keelboat this morning. I jumped in and helped the soldiers load her up, working all in a sweat to get away. I kept thinking I saw Uncle Liam out of the corner of my eye, coming to grab me back.

At last we shoved off. The crew is made up of seven soldiers and two young men besides myself trying out for the Expedition. These two are older, bigger, and stronger than me, but I plan to work twice as hard and take on any extra tasks to make up for what I lack.

An Adventure already!

The boat was scraping sand, so we pulled ashore to shift our load. Folks flocked down to the river to see our odd duck of a boat. While we men unloaded the gear, Capt. Lewis saw a chance to show off his air gun, a modern weapon that delights him no end. He pumped its hollow butt full of air to a high pressure and pulled the trigger. Without any noise or smoke, the gun shot a bullet that hit a target some 50 yards off. Folks cheered. The Captain fired several times. Then he pumped up the gun and handed it to a gentleman to try it for himself, but before the gentleman took aim, he accidentally pulled the trigger. A scream sounded. A lady in the crowd sank to the ground. All of us from the boat ran to where she lay. Blood gushed from her head. I was scared she was dead, but she stirred and sat up. A medical man in the crowd made his way over to her. He said the wound was not deep, but that head wounds always bleed like the dickens. He bound her head with his kerchief. The woman seemed to have no hard feelings. She even waved as we returned to our boat and pulled back into the river.

Evening: Hands blistered bad from oaring.

Ohio River
Sept. 8, '03

My blisters have turned to calluses. My hands are hardened now.

The river is very low. Today we stuck fast on a sandbar. We all hopped out of the boat and unloaded tons of goods—including dozens of heavy iron rods which Capt. Lewis seems particularly attached to. Then some men shoveled a path in the sand while the rest of us stood knee-deep in the cold water, pulling the boat by bow ropes or pushing on the stern. At last we got her over the bar. Then we loaded her up again and rowed down the river to the next sandbar.

Now I know what Capt. Lewis meant by "great bodily fatigue." When we tied up this evening, all the crew moaned over their strained backs. My back is strained, too, but I don't let on. I have never worked so hard. Yet hope of proving myself for the Expedition keeps me jumping.

Ohio River, near Wheeling
Sept. 10, '03

Giant sandbar today. Capt. Lewis sent me trotting to the nearest farmhouse. I asked the farmer if we might rent his horse to help us drag our craft over the shallows.

"Yep," he said. "The going rate is a dollar."

We paid the price, hitched the horse to the boat, and he pulled us over the bar. Tonight the Captain is ranting against this farmer: "Blasted river rat, getting rich off of our hard luck."

Ohio River, south of Wheeling
Sept. 11, '03

Herds of black squirrels swam across the river today. Seaman barked at them, and Capt. Lewis said, "Go!" The dog jumped into the water and paddled swiftly to the squirrels. He snatched one up in his mouth, shook the life out of it, then swam back with it to the Captain. He did this a dozen times. Tonight we fried up those fat squirrels for a fine supper. Seaman got a portion for his trouble.

Most nights, I hold back at supper. I don't want my appetite to count against my being chosen for the Expedition. But tonight there was plenty. How good it felt to eat and eat until I could hold no more!

Ohio River, near Maysville, Kentucky
Sept. 15, '03

We pulled over in a pouring rain to pick up a woodsman, one John Colter. Capt. Lewis sought him out for the Expedition. Colter is known to be a first-rate hunter and tracker. It is hard to see what he looks like, as his face is half hidden behind his red-brown whiskers. His hat, shirt, trousers, and moccasins are all made of buckskin. This evening he seemed to enjoy his whiskey.

I've had no whiskey myself, for I have heard it saps the strength, and I need every bit of what strength I've got.

At last I wrote to Ma. I said Uncle Liam is not the man she thinks he is and begged her not to send Thomas or John to take my place. I told her how I might be picked to go on a great Expedition, and if I am, I will earn a plot of western land for our family. I promised that if not picked, I will go back to Uncle Liam and his shop. Capt. Lewis looked over my shoulder as I wrote.

He seemed pleased, though why I cannot say. One of the soldiers took my letter to the Maysville Post.

Cincinnati
Sept. 30, '03

We have stopped to rest from our 500 mile journey down the Ohio River. In my free time, I sat on shore, making a sketch of the keelboat so that Ma and the others might see the load I have been carrying down the Ohio River. In the end, my drawing fell short, so I tried to capture the keelboat using needle and thread.

Capt. Lewis assigned John Colter and me the task of oiling his precious iron rods, which have rusted. Colter says the rods are for a boat that the Captain dreamed up himself. When we get to the mountains, we will bolt the rods together and cover them with hides to make a boat for sailing down the Columbia River to the Pacific Ocean. Colter calls the iron boat "The Experiment." He says if it ever floats, he will eat his hat, a buckskin affair, darkened with years of sweat, grime, and grease. I have never seen a hat I so admire.

When we docked, the two other young men trying out for the Expedition got off the boat. It is nightfall now. They have not come back. Capt. Lewis thinks the work was too much for them. He asked, "Is the work too much for you, Pup?"

"No, sir," I answered him. "No, *sir*!"

Yet it is hard. Backbreaking hard. Head-throbbing, finger-mashing, blister-raising hard. I don't blame them two for taking off.

Clarksville, Indiana Territory
Oct. 14, '03

We dropped anchor at Clarksville, home to William Clark, who will be a second captain on the Expedition. Capt. Clark rode down to the river to greet us on a red horse that matched his own red hair. This new Captain is tall and big-boned. Capt. Lewis can get all steamed up, but Capt. Clark seems easygoing. The two men served in the army together and seem to think highly of each other.

Capt. Clark is a first-class waterman and has been up and down the Mississippi River many times. He inspected the keelboat from bow to stern.

"Fine-looking boat," he said when he finished. "Fit for the journey."

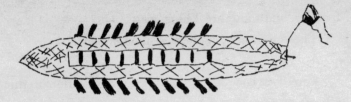

Capt. Clark's slave, York, will go along on the Expedition. York is a big man, tall, broad-shouldered, and dark. Ma and Pa often spoke of the evils of slavery, so I was surprised to hear Capt. Clark say that he and York are the same age and grew up together as brothers.

Tonight York cooked supper, served it to the Captains, then cleared their table. I reckon York must be the brother who does all the work.

Clarksville
Oct. 15, '03

The Captains have picked four Kentucky woodsmen to go on the Expedition.

The first, naturally, is John Colter.

Two woodsman brothers, Reuben and Joseph Fields, were also picked. They look alike, with their brown eyes and brown beards. Capt. Clark has known them for years and calls them "The Boys," though they are both over 30. I watched them shoot. Every one of their bullets hit the target dead center.

Charles Floyd is the fourth. He is only 21, yet was a peacekeeper constable back home. He has sandy hair, freckles, and thoughtful blue eyes.

These four are the luckiest men on earth.

Capt. Lewis wrote a letter to President Jefferson this afternoon. He asked me to copy it over for his records. I did so. The Captain read what I wrote and said, "Well done, Pup."

Clarksville
Oct. 18, '03

Word of the Expedition has spread like wildfire. All who hear of it want to join up and be among the first to explore the vast unknown lands. Every woodsman for 200 miles around has come to Clarksville to try out for it. These new "Hopefuls" are camped near us in the woods. Several gentlemen's sons came, too, but the Captains sent them packing, as they are not used to hard work.

Capt. Clark has lent me a Kentucky rifle. Every morning, we Hopefuls go hunting. When we return, the Captains make a list of who brought in the most game. John Shields's name often tops the list. I have never made the list for, I am sorry to report, as yet I have shot nothing.

Afternoons, the Captains set up footraces, swimming contests, weight-lifting feats, and target-shooting matches. They mark down the names of the winners. I can hold my own in the running and swimming. And even in the lifting, thanks to my time lugging the keelboat over sandbars on the Ohio. Yet I'll never lift half what John Shields can. He is a powerful man, nearly as big as York. Shields is old—35! Yet the Captains do not mind his advanced age, for he is not only strong but also a crack shot and a skilled blacksmith. He is loaded with useful talents for an Expedition.

Writing letters is well and good, but it cannot compare with strong arms and straight shooting. I know I will not be picked. I will never see a flaming volcano. Nor a 7 foot beaver. When the keelboat heads west, I will head back east. Back to Uncle Liam. Back to his head thumps. Back to his threadbare socks. Back to nuts and bolts and barrel hoops. There will be no more miserable young man in all the seventeen United States of America than George Shannon.

Clarksville
Oct. 20, '03

I am picked! I am picked to go!

Capt. Lewis called all Hopefuls together this morning. He announced that in addition to the four men already chosen, he and Capt. Clark had picked five more for the Expedition.

I stood with the hundred other Hopefuls, waiting to hear my fate.

The blacksmith John Shields's name was called.

Next picked was William Bratton, who can mend guns and is a dead-on shot.

George Gibson was chosen. He is good with horses, a fine hunter, and plays the fiddle.

Nathaniel Pryor was picked. He is Charles Floyd's cousin. Floyd told me, anything that gets broke, Nate can fix it.

Then to my great astonishment, Capt. Lewis called out my name. I let out such a whoop of joy that all the men broke up laughing, but I don't care a whit, for I, George Shannon, am going west with the Expedition!

Clarksville
Oct. 21, '03

The nine of us picked took an oath to obey the rules of the U.S. Army. My chest swelled with pride when it came my turn to swear. I aim to prove my worth and never let my Captains down. I am now Private Shannon, 1st United States Regiment, Infantry. If only Pa could see me. Wouldn't he be proud?

After the ceremony, Capt. Lewis slapped me on the back. "Well, Pup," he said. "Looks like you proved yourself all right."

I wanted to ask *what got me picked*, but I could not find the words, so only stood there, grinning like a fool.

I have learned an amazing thing. We will be *paid* to go on this Adventure! As a private in the army, I will earn $5 a month. This money will go into a bank, drawing interest for the two years we expect to be gone.

I wrote to Ma right away. I told her how, in addition

to western land, I will be earning fine pay for this Expedition. I said when I returned, I would bring every cent of it to her. I told Ma she could count on me to do my best to make her proud and to serve my Captains well.

The Captains issued me my own rifle. Colter says if I learn to load her quick, I can fire off two shots a minute! Unless I improve my aim, however, this only means that I will miss more deer.

Capt. Lewis asked me to walk with him a spell. As we tramped through the woods, he told me that he will keep the Scientific Notebook as we go. Capt. Clark will make the book of maps. All Expedition officers will keep journals. He said he noticed that I already kept a journal. I told him Ma had sent the journal to me. That I wrote in it faithfully so that Ma and the others back home might one day read of my Adventure.

Hearing this, Capt. Lewis got all worked up, the way he does. "That's it, Pup!" he said. "Write your story, a private's story, of the Expedition!" He said I must put down exactly how I see things. He said he would never ask to read my journal. That it would exist for posterity, that was what mattered. He went on and on, and I lost him in parts. He finished by saying, "Write a true and honest story, Pup. Tell how you left your home and your family, how you left America and all that you knew to voyage out into the Great Unknown!"

Naturally I said, "Yes, sir!"

Fort Massac
Nov. 11, '03

We stopped to pick up an Indian-language interpreter, one George Drewyer. (That makes three Georges and several Johns, so everyone is to be called by their last name. I am called Shannon, except by Capt. Lewis, who still says Pup.)

Drewyer's pa is French. His ma is Shawnee. Drewyer speaks English, French, Shawnee, and many other Indian languages. He also knows the hand signs that Indians use to talk among themselves when they have no common tongue. Drewyer puts me in mind of a great bear. He has dark eyes and hair, which he wears in two long braids. He is known to be able to track anything that moves. With him on board, our Expedition cannot help but succeed.

At this fort, we also picked up two soldiers, John Newman and Joseph Whitehouse, another tailor.

Ohio River
Nov. 13, '03

We shoved off from Fort Massac in a rainstorm. Shortly after, Capt. Lewis came down with chills and a fever. He put Seaman in my care, and the dog hunkered down beneath my knees as I rowed. Capt. Lewis swallowed several pills he got from a Dr. Rush in Philadelphia. He called the pills Thunder Clappers, as they cause quite an uproar of the bowels. Then he shut himself inside the boat's cabin with a chamber pot and stayed for a long spell. When at last he came out, he was pale but said he felt better, having emptied his system.

Meeting of the Ohio and Mississippi Rivers
Nov. 16, '03

We dropped anchor near a camp of Shawnees. Charles Floyd and I got off the boat with Capt. Lewis. We carried the instruments for measuring where we are by taking what the Captain calls celestial observations. Naturally Seaman came along.

The sky was blue with not a cloud in it. I said what a fine sky, but Capt. Lewis said I should set up the gear and be quick about it. No sooner was it up than Capt. Lewis said by his watch, it was noon, on the dot. At that very moment, he took his Octant and measured how high the sun was in the sky. Then he riffled through a book to a chart, where knowing the exact time of day, the angle of the sun, and the date tells him how far north we are from the equator. Capt. Lewis repeated this process many times over. The man is never happier than when he is measuring.

A Shawnee brave watched us work. With the Captain's permission, he threw sticks into the river for Seaman to fetch. The dog is a great show-off, and he swam tirelessly back and forth.

We finished our task and were packing up when the Shawnee held out three beaver pelts. He signed, and his meaning was clear: He wished to trade them for the dog. I froze. I feared this might be the last I saw of Seaman, for three beaver pelts are worth many times over $20, but Capt. Lewis shook his head. On the way back to the boat, I was glad to hear him say that no amount of beaver pelts could ever part him from his dog.

Wood River
Dec. 13, '03

We are camped on a high bluff beside small Wood River, overlooking the wide Mississippi River. Here, on the very western edge of the United States of America, we will build our winter fort.

When I look across the Mississippi, I can see St. Louis, a city of some one thousand people, mostly French. Beyond the city is a wilderness called Louisiana Territory, owned by the French. This territory is home to many Indian nations and some French traders and settlers. Directly across the river from our camp is the wide mouth of the Missouri River. Come spring, we will paddle up her.

***

I helped cut down trees for building our huts and a sheltered privy. Squatting out in the snow will soon be a thing of the past!

Later Charles Floyd and I walked to Wood River to collect drinking water. We are the youngest men on the Expedition. As we went, Floyd said, "Back home, my friends call me Charlie. I would be pleased if you called me Charlie, too."

"I will," I said, "and you must call me George."

A pioneer settlement is nearby. We had hardly pulled ashore when John Colter paid the pioneers a visit. He came back, saying he met some very fine folk.

Capt. Clark suffers from a sore throat. York asked me to fetch a bolt of red flannel, intended as a gift for the Indians. He wrapped a length of it around the Captain's neck. He says red flannel worn next to the skin will cure any cold.

Fort Wood River
Dec. 23, '03

John Colter is neighborly. He visits those pioneers most every day.

My shirttails have worn so thin, there is hardly enough to wrap around my private parts before I pull on my trousers. I am feeling the cold.

25

Fort Wood River
Dec. 24, '03

When we slept out in the open, I never heard anyone snore. Last night we moved into our huts, and the chorus of snores would have drowned out a thunderstorm.

Fort Wood River
Christmas Day, '03

Awakened at dawn by Colter and others firing off their guns in celebration.

I tramped through the snowy woods all day with a party of hunters. George Drewyer and George Gibson shot several deer and wild turkeys. (Sad to say, I am the only George who shot nothing this Christmas.) We brought the game back to camp, and York cooked up a feast. Shields surprised us by bringing cheese and butter to the table. Oh, how good it tasted!

Colter shot four deer. He took the meat to the pioneers for their Christmas dinner, so he missed our feast. A more generous man would be hard to find.

Fort Wood River
Dec. 28, '03

Capt. Lewis spends much time in St. Louis, meeting with traders who paddle up the Missouri River to do business with the Indians we hope to meet. He copies their maps. When he returns to the fort, he and Capt. Clark spend hours bent over these maps.

When Capt. Lewis is away, I look after Seaman. The dog accepts me as a second master now. He follows me and sleeps at my feet, warming me more than an extra blanket.

As we sat round the fire tonight, John Colter took out needle and thread. He began sewing a pair of breeches cut from the hide of a deer he shot. I got my red leather kit and joined him in stitching, lining my worn-out shirttails with pieces of red flannel.

Fort Wood River
Dec. 30, '03

Seventeen army soldiers are in our party now. They are led by Sergeant John Ordway from New Hampshire, a serious sort.

One of the soldiers, John Collins, offered a bet that he could walk the whole way round the fort on his hands, never stopping. He had many takers. Yesterday, with all looking on, he sprang onto his hands and padded round the fort as easy as if walking on a pair of feet. Colter paid his money to Collins without complaining, but later he told me he will find a way to win it back.

Capt. Lewis is pacing tonight, muttering of liars and maps. He has copied out an old trader's map of the western Missouri River. The old trader swears it is accurate. If it is, then we will have to travel a short distance on land from the source of the Missouri River to the source of the Columbia. The old trader told Capt. Lewis that he crossed this stretch himself in half a day with the help of several fine horses bought from the Shoshone Indians, who live nearby. Half a day's journey is not so bad. Still, Capt. Lewis believes this old trader is mistaken. He says he will find the Northwest Passage.

Fort Wood River
Jan. 1, 1804

We have daily target practice. Each man gets only one shot, as we must save ammunition. Today I missed the target entirely. No one said a word, but it weighs heavy on me.

Fort Wood River
Jan. 6, '04

Rainy. I came into the hut and found Collins drawing a sketch of Colter. It showed him running, with his hat falling off and his hair flying out behind. His face was all whiskers, and two beady eyes. Collins held up another sketch. Right off I knew it was Shields. The drawing showed a man with enormous muscles and a hammer in his hand. He looked like some sort of thunder god, which Shields more or less resembles. I told Collins that he had a great talent for likeness. He held up a third picture. It showed a lanky lad with sprouting hair, wide eyes, and an eager grin on his face. His pants were too short. His shirtsleeves hit way above the wrist. He was holding out a plate, as if begging for food. I asked Collins if this was some boyhood friend.

"No, sir," he said. "It is a drawing of Private G. Shannon."

I couldn't see a bit of likeness in it. Yet there was Seaman at my side, and Collins had captured the dog entirely.

I paid Colter 50¢ for one of his deer hides. I am stitching up a pair of pants long enough to reach my ankles.

Fort Wood River
Jan. 7, '04

I helped two of the soldiers, Hugh McNeal and Patrick Gass, chop down six monstrous big cottonwoods today. Gass is a skilled carpenter. He will head up a team building supply boats for our journey out of these trees.

Fort Wood River
Jan. 8, '04

Capt. Clark was out talking to the guard last night when Colter came back from the pioneers. It seems that Colter was walking none too steady, and the Captain discovered that his visits to the settlement have been spent entirely in its tavern. The settlement is now off limits to all men.

Fort Wood River
Jan. 9, '04

Collins came in from hunting with a load of bear meat. He roasted it on a spit and served it for our supper. I had never eaten bear before, and was surprised to find the meat flavorful and tender. Seaman sat near me as I ate. I thought back to the time I mistook him for a bear on the Pittsburgh wharf, and gave him some scraps, for if it weren't for Seaman, I would not be here now.

Fort Wood River
Jan. 10, '04

A man stormed into camp today, waving a knife and making a great fuss, all in French. Drewyer told us he was saying he had butchered a hog, hung it up, and now it was gone. Capt. Clark found Collins, and Collins confessed that his "bear" was indeed this same hog. From here on out, Collins must take all the game he shoots to the Frenchman.

Fort Wood River
Jan. 19, '04

Yesterday Capt. Clark went for a ramble on the ice and

froze his feet. This morning he woke up with a chest cold. York is fixing him duck soup. The smell of it cooking makes me half wish for a chest cold of my own.

Snow blankets the ground. It looks harmless, but I know better. It can freeze a man in no time. This is Ma's first winter without Pa. How sad she must feel, looking out at the snow.

Fort Wood River
Jan. 20, '04

Capt. Lewis bought a bronze cannon in St. Louis. Charlie and I worked with John Potts, one of the soldiers, to fasten it to the bow of the keelboat, mounted on a swivel so it can turn easily and fire in any direction. It can shoot a 1 pound cannonball or sixteen musket balls all at once.

We next fixed two large shotguns to the stern. Capt. Lewis calls them blunderbusses. These guns can be loaded with musket balls or scrap iron—nails and such. We aim to put a blunderbuss on each of the supply boats, too. We will be floating forts!

Fort Wood River
Jan. 21, '04

More snow. Charlie and I are helping Patrick Gass build storage lockers inside the keelboat. They will hold our cargo. If attacked, we can raise the locker lids for shields.

Most of our cargo will be gifts for the Indians. We

will give the chief of each nation a U.S. military uniform—a red coat, leggings, and a three-cornered hat with a feather plume. We will also give out silver peace medals and U.S. flags. Capt. Lewis says these gifts will help the chiefs feel a part of the United States. To the people of each nation, we will give useful items, such as wool blankets, axes, knives, scissors, needles, thimbles, fishhooks, kettles, corn grinders, and burning glasses for starting fires with sunlight. We will also give twists of tobacco and gewgaws, such as rings with glass stones, silk ribbons, hair combs, and red and blue beads. Capt. Lewis says that in the west, beads are valued higher than money.

Capt. Clark says what Indians truly want are rifles, balls, and gunpowder, but we will not be giving these.

Fort Wood River
Jan. 22, '04

Charlie and I are packing up the Indian presents. (My time apprenticed to Uncle Liam made me an expert at counting and sorting!) We mark each bundle with the name of an Indian nation. Going up the Missouri River, Capt. Lewis says we expect to meet, in this order:

1. *Oto*
2. *Missouri*
3. *Omaha*
4. *Yankton Sioux*
5. *Teton Sioux*

6. *Arikara*

7. *Mandan*

8. *Hidatsa*

All are said to be friendly to Americans, except the Teton Sioux.

We also have five unmarked gift bales for Indians we may meet in Parts Unknown.

Fort Wood River
Jan. 24, '04

Capt. Clark found a hammer that was left out in the rain all night. He held it up, asking who had been using it. With a jolt, I realized it was me and owned up to the deed. How could I be so careless? I am sanding and oiling the hammer to rid it of rust.

Fort Wood River
Jan. 25, '04

Capt. Clark coughed all night.

Fort Wood River
Jan. 27, '04

Capt. Clark's throat and chest are now wrapped in red flannel, yet his cold is worse. Capt. Lewis is treating him with Dr. Rush's walnut-bark pills to empty out his system.

Rainy evening. Sat inside the damp, smoky hut. It smelled strongly of woodsmen. Joe Whitehouse was mending his breeches. Colter was patching his moccasins. None of my clothes are holey, but I got out my red kit and began stitching a map. When finished, it will show the route I took with Capt. Lewis from Pittsburgh, down the Ohio River, and up the Mississippi to Fort Wood River.

Fort Wood River
Jan. 30, '04

Capt. Lewis is all worked up about how our corps must march for the Indians we meet to show off our skill and discipline. We have marching practice every day. The soldiers hired for the Expedition do not seem to mind walking in step and turning all at the same time, but the Kentucky boys grumble. I would rather dig a privy than march. Joseph Fields says he would not have joined up if he knew he had to go parading. When we drill, Charlie and I must keep our eyes off of Colter, for the sight of him marching is so comical that twice we broke up laughing and got a reprimand.

Capt. Clark's nose never stops running. The flannel wrap has not helped his throat. Capt. Lewis has doubled up on his bark pills.

***

All the Indian gift bales are packed in the keelboat lockers. The supply boats are painted—one red, one white. We are raring to go but cannot shove off until spring. Now we have time on our hands. Today Colter challenged Collins to a tobacco-spitting contest. Collins accepted. The men set a bucket at the base of a cottonwood tree. Each took a plug of tobacco, bit off a quid, chewed, then took turns spewing deep brown gobs of spit into the bucket. After every round, they backed up a step until finally Collins missed. In this way, Colter won his money back.

I use my free time to teach Seaman tricks. He can sit, give a paw, roll over, and chase his tail, all on command. I am also stitching a buckskin hat modeled on Colter's. And Drewyer is teaching me hand signs for talking with the Indians.

The Captains have been invited to a fancy-dress ball in St. Louis. Capt. Clark says his cold will not stand in the way of his going. York has unpacked his blue uniform coat and his three-cornered hat with the white plume. He says he only hopes that the Captain will not be foolish enough to bathe before the ball, as it would put his health at risk.

We men are not invited. This is just as well. I would not know what to do with myself at a ball. Still, I would like to see St. Louis.

The tailor Joe Whitehouse showed me how to stitch a deerskin possible bag for carrying personal items. When I finished mine, I loaded it up with my toothbrush, soap, pewter mug, tin mirror, straight razor (which I use every week now), tinderbox, burning glass, compass, eagle-feather quills, six papers of ink powder, and one walnut-shell inkwell. I made it big enough to hold my housewife kit and this journal, too. With such a bag of tricks, I am prepared for any possible situation.

Fort Wood River
Feb. 23, '04

Today the military uniforms that Capt. Lewis ordered for us woodsmen arrived. We tried them on. My blue trousers are comfortable enough, but my brown wool jacket with pewter buttons is heavy as lead. I am glad it will be mostly packed away and worn only when we show off for the Indians. I tried to put on the boots sent for me, but could not squeeze my feet into them. Capt. Lewis grumbled about my paws growing but says he will send for a bigger pair.

Seeing us in our uniforms, Capt. Lewis ordered all

men to shave their beards. I don't have many whiskers, but shaved what I could.

Colter and the Fields brothers came to supper shaved. Colter looks particularly naked.

Fort Wood River
Feb. 25, '04

Both Captains went off to St. Louis for the ball and to gather supplies, leaving Sgt. Ordway in charge. Last night the Sergeant ordered Shields and Reuben Fields to stand guard, but they said they'd be damned if they'd take orders from him. Instead they went out "hunting" with Colter and some others. I was standing guard at 3:00 this morning when they came back, singing and firing off their guns.

Fort Wood River
March 3, '04

When Capt. Lewis returned and learned what had gone on during his absence, he lined up the whole party.

"All who went to the pioneer settlement are confined to camp for ten days," he told us. "Capt. Clark and I must both be away at times. When we are not here, Sgt. Ordway is the officer in charge. In the future, disobedience to him will be dealt with by military court-martial."

I believe he means some sort of a trial.

Fort Wood River
March 12, '04

Capt. Lewis made another trip to St. Louis. He returned singing and tossing his hat in the air. When Seaman ran to greet him, he threw his arms around the dog and swung him in a dance. His good spirits came from attending a ceremony where the French flag was lowered and the U.S. flag raised over Louisiana Territory. It seems that Napoleon, the emperor of France, was afraid that the British would capture Louisiana Territory from him, so he sold it

Missouri River

Fort Wood River

St. Louis

Fort
Massac

Mississippi River

Ohio River

to the United States for $15 million. Capt. Lewis is delighted. This territory includes the Missouri River and all its forks and branches. Now the Expedition will be traveling in American territory all the way to the Rocky

Pittsburgh

Shannon Farm
(my home)

Wheeling

Cincinnati

Maysville

Clarksville

Mountains. Capt. Lewis says when we meet Indians, we will tell them they now live on American soil.

Tonight Drewyer told me that Indians do not believe that land can belong to any one nation.

I finished stitching my map. One of the soldiers,

Moses Reed, said it looks like an ailing snake, but others admired it.

Fort Wood River
March 29, '04

Both Captains are away again.

Last night I was jolted out of a dead sleep by men shouting. I ran out of the hut to find Shields shaking his fist at Sgt. Ordway, who was in charge.

"We are going to the pioneer settlement!" Shields yelled.

"And no Yankee sergeant is going to stop us!" added Frazer, one of the soldiers.

"You try it," said Colter, waving his rifle at the sergeant, "and I'll blow your head off!"

Charlie was trying to calm everyone. At last he succeeded, and Colter put down his gun.

This morning, the three felt bad for their deeds. They begged Sgt. Ordway to forgive them, and he obliged.

The Captains are back. They say they will not punish the three because they apologized. It is lucky for Shields that he is a master blacksmith. And for Colter that he is a dead-on shot. Otherwise, things might have gone differently for them.

If we can't get along in camp, how will we do on the long voyage ahead?

Supplies arrive from St. Louis every day: pork, hard biscuits, dried corn, flour, beans, salt, sugar, coffee, whiskey. Also hundreds of pounds of what Capt. Lewis calls "portable soup." This is made of vegetables, mostly beans, dried out and crushed to a powder. Charlie and I mixed some with boiling water and had a taste. The broth was the color of mud and tasted no better, but we said nothing to Capt. Lewis, as he seems so pleased with his soup.

The waiting is hard now. I ache to get going.

Fine news for Charlie! The Captains made him a sergeant. He is a born leader, even though young. His cousin, Nathaniel Pryor, was also made a sergeant. Sgt. Ordway will keep his rank. As officers, sergeants are ordered to keep journals of the Expedition.

Our Expedition party is now complete with 2 captains, 3 sergeants, and 22 privates. We also have 1 slave, York. And 1 interpreter, Drewyer. And, I should add, 1 dog. Capt. Lewis calls us the Corps of Discovery.

The Captains put us privates into squads under the three sergeants. I am in Sgt. Pryor's squad, along with Shields, Gibson, and Whitehouse. Four soldiers are also in this squad: Collins, Howard, Weiser, and Hall. Sgt. Pryor is sick today. Capt. Lewis wrote in his order book that "while Sgt. Pryor is ill, Geo. Shannon is appointed to lead his Squad." I am proud to be a squad leader, even if only temporary.

Fort Wood River
April 2, '04

The Captains gathered us together to explain their plan for our journey. We twenty-two privates will row the keelboat. One Captain will ride in the keelboat while the other walks along on shore. The smaller boats, or pirogues as the French watermen call them, will follow us, carrying supplies. Six French watermen have been hired to crew the white pirogue. Six soldiers under the command of Corporal Warfington will crew the red one. In this way, we will travel up the Missouri, hoping to reach the Mandan villages before winter sets in.

If the Mandan are friendly, we will build our winter fort near them. Over the winter, we privates will cut down trees and make dugout canoes. Next spring, the Corps will paddle these canoes and the pirogues up to the beginning of the Missouri River in the mountains. Then, if that old trader is right and we must travel by land a short distance, we will buy Shoshone horses, load up our goods, and lead them to the Columbia River. There we will join together the iron skeleton of Capt. Lewis's boat, cover its frame with elk hide, and sail to the Pacific Ocean.

Fort Wood River
April 6, '04

The Captains gave each man a bone-handled knife and a tomahawk. They warned us not to lose them, as they cannot be replaced on the journey. They also gave us each gunpowder and one hundred rifle bullets.

Fort Wood River
April 12, '04

I cannot find my bone-handled knife.

Fort Wood River
April 17, '04

My knife is still missing. I have looked everywhere for it but no luck. Can there be a thief in camp?

Good news! Capt. Clark has ordered Charlie and me to take two horses to Capt. Lewis in St. Louis tomorrow.

Fort Wood River
April 19, '04

Still dark when Charlie and I rode the horses onto the

ferry. The sun rose as we crossed the Mississippi, turning the whitewashed houses of St. Louis pink in the early light.

We landed at a wharf packed with merchants and fur traders. They were shouting, all at the same time, in all sorts of languages. Charlie had never been to a city before. He was at a loss as to how we might find Capt. Lewis. My time in Pittsburgh came in handy, and I was able to follow our directions to the home of Capt. Stoddard, governor of the territory. We found Capt. Lewis there and turned the horses over to him.

Capt. Lewis sent Charlie and me to the city's doctor to pick up a box of medicines. The doctor also gave us a pack of matches. He struck one of the small sticks against a rough stone. Its sulfur-treated head burst into flame! This will be a most handy item to have along on our journey.

Charlie and I carried the medical supplies to the ferry and rode back across the river. Seaman was on the bank when we docked. Whitehouse said the dog had sat there all day, waiting.

Fort Wood River
May 2, '04

The thief is caught! Last evening, Seaman dug up what I took to be a bone. I looked closer and found it was my bone-handled knife. The blade was rusted, but

nothing a little elbow grease can't fix. When the knife
is clean, I will carve my initials into the handle: G.S.

Fort Wood River
May 5, '04

The rivers are flooded from heavy spring rains. Moses
Reed and I were sent for kindling, and we stopped a
minute, watching the brown waters of the Missouri
River come racing and frothing into the Mississippi.
The violent spray spewed out whole uprooted trees as
if they were no more than toothpicks. Reed says the
Captains are out of their minds to think we can row up
this river. I don't like to agree with Reed, who never has
a good word to say, but when I see the wild waters, I
wonder—can we do it?

Fort Wood River
May 9, '04

Hot. We loaded the keelboat and took her out on the
Mississippi and rowed her 8 miles for a test. The boat
rocked badly the whole way.

"Loaded too heavy in the bow," Capt. Clark said
when we pulled her ashore. We unloaded the boat
and packed her up again. It was hard, sweaty work.
We struggled to fit the long iron bars of "The Experiment" into the lockers. At last Capt. Clark said we had

the balance right for going upriver, with the heavy cargo in the stern.

Missouri River Island
May 14, '04

Good-bye, Wood River! We shoved off this afternoon, all of us in high spirits in spite of the pouring rain. Some neighbors turned out to wave their caps and holler farewell. One man wept as he waved. Charlie said he must be the tavern keeper from the pioneer settlement, crying over parting from John Colter.

I sat on a bench beside Whitehouse, pulling my oar in time with the others. Rowing across the Mississippi was hard. Then we started up the Missouri, and oh, how we strained at our oars against the raging current. We kept at it all afternoon, but made only 4 miles.

Now camped on an island in the middle of the river. Every muscle in my body aches. My oar wasn't sanded proper, so I have spent the evening with a stitching needle, picking out splinters.

It is still raining. But at last our Adventure is begun!

Missouri River Island
May 15, '04

Awakened before dawn by Sgt. Ordway tooting his bugle. We struck our tents, packed our bedrolls in the keelboat, and shoved off. Hard going on account of huge trees washed into the river by spring floods. Their roots have sunk into the muddy river bottom, but their sharp branches stick up just under the surface of the water, making them hard to spot. These branches swing back and forth in the current with a sawing motion, so they are called sawyers. Our boat got stuck on three of these sawyers today. Each time we came near to overturning but saved ourselves by jamming our poles into the river bottom and pushing with all our might to lift her free.

Charlie asked Capt. Clark why we got snagged up so many times today.

Capt. Clark said, "Loaded too heavy in the stern."

St. Charles
May 16, '04

Dropped anchor at St. Charles. Villagers, mainly French and Indian, ran down to greet us. One young French lady with dark curls waved at me. I waved back. She and a friend stayed and watched us unload the boat. Then we packed her up again, putting more weight in the bow. While we worked, Charlie and I joked about "accidentally" dropping Capt. Lewis's iron boat frame overboard.

Capt. Lewis is all worked up. He has hired an expert Missouri River lookout for the Expedition. He says this man can spot the devilish "sawyers" lurking under the current in time to steer us clear of them. We are badly in need of such an expert.

Has Capt. Lewis lost his mind? I saw the "expert" lookout he hired. He has only one eye!

I have met the expert, Pierre Cruzatte. He wears a leather patch over his left eye. Yet Drewyer says his right eye is the sharpest on the river, and his opinion is good enough for me. Cruzatte is small and wiry. He is part French and part Omaha, so he can also act as an interpreter. I was glad to see that he brought his fiddle aboard. Another French and Indian boatman, François Labiche, was hired as well. We all stood round while they were sworn in as privates. That makes twenty-four.

The Captains bought two horses. One is gray. The other is brown with a white star on her chest. They will be led along shore as we go. We can ride them out hunting, and they can carry any large game we shoot back to the boat. Colter spoke up and named the gray horse Mary Jane. He named the brown one Lizzy. He says he named them in honor of two young ladies whose hearts he broke by going off on the Expedition. Charlie and I had ourselves a laugh, picturing John Colter a ladies' man!

Near midnight: The St. Charles villagers cleared the streets and threw us a ball to send us off on our Adventure.

Fiddlers fiddled and we danced for hours, all lining up and swinging one partner after another. I had a fine time dancing the Virginia Reel with the dark-haired young French lady. Her name is Marie-Claire. Aside from her name, I could not understand a word she said, so I asked Drewyer to translate.

"Marie-Claire says she hopes you will stop by St. Charles again on your way home," he said.

Is Drewyer pulling my leg?

Hall, Warner, and Collins were assigned to guard the boat this evening, but they left their post and crashed the ball. Collins cut up, acting wild, and dancing on his hands. The three have not yet come back to the boat.

St. Charles
May 17, '04

The Captains set up a court-martial for Hall, Warner, and Collins. Sgt. Ordway and four privates put on their dress uniforms to act as jury. Hall and Warner pled guilty to going absent without leave and were sentenced to receive twenty-five lashes on their bare backs. But as they had not behaved badly in the past, the Captains said this could be a warning. They will not carry out the sentence.

Poor Collins! The jury found him guilty of three

crimes. Because of that time he stole the hog, he did not get off so easy. This evening at sunset, he will get fifty lashes.

I chose not to watch the whipping. Charlie said it was awful, but Collins bore it like a man.

St. Charles
May 21, '04

Capt. Stoddard offered to take letters to the postmaster in St. Louis, so most of us wrote home one last time. Writing in this journal goes so easy, but writing to Ma was hard. I pictured her gentle face and steady gaze and got such an ache that I came near to sniveling. At last I wrote that I am in good health and good spirits and hope she and all the little ones will keep safe over the two years we are apart. I gave my letter to Capt. Stoddard.

I have cast my lot with Capt. Lewis and his great Expedition!

We are about to shove off. Is that Marie-Claire, waving?

Missouri River
May 23, '04

Dicey going today. I learned that not all trees uprooted by the spring rains sink down to become sawyers. No, sir.

Some float on the current and come barreling down the river at astonishing speeds. If one of these trees were to hit us, it would bash a hole in our hull and sink us fast.

Our expert Pierre Cruzatte stood lookout in the bow, armed with an iron-tipped pole. When he spied a tree headed for us, he ran over, thrust his pole at it, and shoved it away. I have never seen a man move quicker.

Yet some of the floating timbers were too big even for our expert. We had just got under way when Cruzatte spied a monster coming right for our boat. He blew a blast on his tin horn. This was a signal to us rowers to jump up and rush to the side of the boat where he pointed. All together we thrust our oars at the wooden giant, shoving it away from the boat. When the danger was past, we had hardly sat back down to row when Cruzatte tooted his horn and up we jumped again.

This dance never let up all day. Twice we came close to overturning, but Pierre Cruzatte's warnings saved us just in time. Colter has taken to calling him Saint Peter.

Seaman did not like today's wild ride. He slunk into the cabin and never came out until we pulled ashore to make camp.

I lost two oars fighting those logs. A soldier, Alex Willard, lost one. That makes me feel some better, but now we have no extras.

Capt. Lewis is shaken by these close calls. He says from here on out, I must stash my journal with his, in a tin box with a tight-fitting lid that holds enough air to make it float. Then, he says, should the worst happen, at least our words will be saved for posterity.

I went out with the hunting party this evening. Everyone shot a deer but me. I am so ashamed to have brought in no food for the party.

Devil's Race Ground, Missouri River
May 24, '04

We hit a narrow stretch of river called Devil's Race Ground. When I saw how violent the current ran, I thought it rightly named. I was glad to hear Capt. Clark say we could not row it, but must "pole and pull." Charlie and I grabbed poles. We stabbed them into the river bottom, leaned on those poles with all our strength, and pushed the boat ahead. Others jumped into the water. They took hold of the tow ropes and began to pull the boat through the bad spot. Just when I thought we had passed the worst, the current wheeled the boat around so fast, the tow ropes snapped. The jolt tossed me into the river. I lost my pole but managed to swim back to the boat. I grabbed on and helped hold her upright in the current, while others dove under to try to hook up a rope. At last they succeeded, but the boat nearly swamped three more times before we got her through the devilish pass.

Afterward, Capt. Clark said, "Worst stretch of river I ever laid eyes on."

Tonight, around the campfire, Gibson confessed to the Captains that he cannot swim. John Potts piped up and said the same. Later I went to Capt. Lewis in the keelboat cabin to write some letters for him. I found him muttering, "They signed up for two years on the water, and they cannot *swim*?"

Gibson and the others were scared by Devil's Race Ground. Yet I understand why they signed on. Even though they might be drowned, they did not want to miss this chance for Adventure.

I write by starlight and embers. The Captains are bedded down in the keelboat. Seaman prefers to sleep on land, so sticks with me at night, even when I take my turn standing guard. The French watermen have a campfire burning down the beach, not far from where the three sergeants are camped. We privates have our own campfire. York came and sat with us a spell. He told us he has a wife, yet hardly sees her, as she is owned by another master. When the men began to turn in, York went off and spread his bedroll near the keelboat, close enough to hear Capt. Clark, should he call. Around the campfire, I forget that York is not one of us privates, but he is not. He is a slave, owned by Capt. Clark. How sad and lonely for York.

La Charette
May 25, '04

We stopped at the last white settlement on the river. From here on out, we will be traveling in Indian territory.

The La Charette settlers ran down to the river to see our boat. They seemed impressed with it. And with Seaman. I swear, that dog was smiling as he showed off his fetching skills.

Capt. Lewis often walks on shore as the boats go up-river. This afternoon he asked me to walk with him, and in my company, he worried out loud.

"Our party makes a tempting target, Pup," he said. "If any Indian nation were to rob us of our guns and ammunition, they could easily rule all other tribes. From what I am told, the Teton Sioux would like to do just that."

The Captains announced plans to keep us safe. From here on out, we will make camp on islands in the river. We will rotate guard duty. One sergeant and six privates will always be watching the boats. If there is a surprise attack, the guards will blow the tin horns to wake the rest of the party. Our weapons are to be always loaded and ready.

Seaman has caught our wary mood. His ears perk up at the slightest sound.

Thunderstorm this morning. We rowed all day against strong winds. By the time we stopped for the night, our bellies were growling.

At supper, Capt. Lewis told us that by his account, each man eats some 9 pounds of meat a day. "And we can double that for the Pup," he said with a nod in my direction. Everyone laughed. I felt my face grow warm. If only I were bringing in some meat!

Went hunting with Reuben and Joseph Fields this evening. I asked them to show me any trick that might improve my aim. Reuben told me once I spot a deer, never to take my eye off it even to blink, but to raise my gun up to my eye. I tried this. No luck. Still, I keep hoping.

Mouth of the Gasconade River
May 27, '04

I shot a deer! The smell of it roasting over the cook fire made my mouth water. Colter, Collins, Drewyer, Whitehouse, Shields, Gibson, and the Fields brothers all came round and slapped me on the back. I think they have been hoping for this day as much as I have. Seaman is gnawing on the hock. He seems to enjoy this bone more than most.

Missouri River
May 28, '04

We have been on our journey fourteen days, seven of them rainy. Today the sun came out. We stopped, unloaded our wet baggage, and aired it out.

Sundown: It is raining.

Mouth of the Osage River
June 3, '04

Capt. Clark is never without his red flannel neck scarf, yet his cold lingers on.

Missouri River
June 4, '04

I have not felt so low since my days of sorting nails for Uncle Liam.

Sgt. Ordway asked me to steer the boat for a spell. I took the tiller, but steering was not as easy as it looked, and I brought the bow too near the shore. Seeing this, Sgt. Ordway grabbed for the tiller, but too late. A rope on the mast got caught in the branches of a sycamore.

The mast stuck fast and, as the boat moved forward, it snapped in two. Now we have no mast. We cannot raise our sail. This means more rowing for everyone. And more work, too, for we must find a tall tree and make a new mast. Capt. Lewis never said a harsh word to me about it, but how foolish of me to take the tiller when I had never steered before. I try not to look up as we go, for when I do, I see the stump of what was once our mast.

Missouri River
June 5, '04

Our hunters brought in eight deer. Charlie and I cut the extra meat into thin strips. We laid it out in the sun to dry. We now have jerky for travel rations.

Herds of mosquitoes swarm around us. At night we roll up in mosquito curtains so the buzzing varmints cannot get at us. But all day as we row, they chew us without mercy.

Seaman is plagued by ticks. I picked dozens out of his coat last night, but dozens more clamped on to him today.

Capt. Clark's throat is paining him. York says greens will restore his health. This evening he swam to a sandbar to gather watercress, which he served to the Captain at supper.

***

We found a fine straight tree for a mast. Charlie and I cut it down. Sgt. Pryor and Gass are working to shape it. Every minute I am not rowing or poling, I help with the mast.

Capt. Clark asked me to walk with him on shore this afternoon. He carried his umbrella as he went to shield his fair skin from the sun. We came upon a den of poisonous rattlesnakes. Capt. Clark shot three of them. We cut the rattles from their tails and have brought them back to the boat, as they are said to be powerful medicine.

Today as we rowed, Labiche called out, "Pirogue ahead!" And here came three trappers heading downriver in a boat loaded with beaver pelts. We all pulled ashore for a parley.

The men spent a year up north, hunting and trapping, and are headed to St. Louis to sell their furs. They said they started out with many more pelts, but when they paddled by a Teton Sioux village, armed warriors rowed out to their boat and demanded half their goods. The trappers were outnumbered and, in the end, gave up the pelts to save their own hides. They warned the Captains: Beware the Teton river pirates.

The trappers went on down the river. Capt. Lewis

muttered, "I'll be damned if our Expedition will be stopped by pirates."

Arrow Rock
June 9, '04

We rammed a sawyer and stuck fast on a pointed branch. The rapids swung the boat around so our broad side faced the current. At that same moment, two huge trees came barreling down the river toward us, and Saint Peter called out, "Timbers ahead!" We all quick jumped out of the boat and grabbed the tow ropes. By heaving hard, we got her loose from the sawyer only seconds before the timbers would have hit.

Gibson near drowned today. My hands are bloody from gripping the tow rope. I lost another oar. But our boat is saved. Capt. Clark says our party is equal to the best crew he ever saw on the Mississippi.

Since we left St. Charles, there have been no fights. No one has given the Captains any trouble. It is as if we have all banded together to fight the wild, raging Missouri River.

Night: Rain comes down in buckets. No way to make a fire, so we dined on dried corn and hogs' lard. After the Captains bedded down in the boat, Moses Reed complained that no one told him the journey would be so hard.

I know what he means. No one told us mosquitoes

would chew us half to death. Nor that we would strain our backs and bloody our hands. Yet no one told us of the deep satisfaction that comes from sitting on a bench, rowing in time with the others of our Corps. Nor how good it feels at the end of a day to put down our oars. Nor of the taste of fresh deer meat roasted over a campfire. Nor of lying back on a clear night, watching stars shoot through the skies.

Will Bratton spoke up. "Reed," he said, "a thousand woodsmen back in Kentucky would give their right arms to be where you are now."

Reed only sulked, but the rest of us nodded. I would not have missed this trip for the world.

Missouri River
June 10, '04

At last the rain has stopped. There is plenty of game here. Our bellies are full, and we are in good health and good spirits. Tonight by the fire, Saint Peter and Gibson played their fiddles. We men hooked elbows and swung round and round. After the dancing, I started singing "Get Along Home, Cindy, Cindy." All the men chimed in on the chorus. Then Collins jumped up. He sang some verses of his own, each one wickeder than the last. It seems the Fields brothers did not know this song had such possibilities, and they laughed themselves silly.

Missouri River
June 12, '04

Two French pirogues paddled down the river this afternoon carrying voyagers' grease made from hard buffalo fat called tallow. The Frenchmen say the grease is good for cooking or can be slathered on the skin to ward off mosquitoes. Capt. Lewis bought 300 pounds of it. I would never rub such stinking stuff onto my skin, but Seaman sniffs round the greasy barrel, drooling.

Capt. Lewis hired one of the Frenchmen from the pirogues to translate our talks with the Yankton Sioux. He gave his name as Old Dorion. His skin is as brown and wrinkled as the bark of a tree. His wife is a Yankton Sioux, and he has lived among her people for twenty years. We are lucky to have run across Old Dorion.

Missouri River
June 15, '04

Swift current. We towed the boat with ropes. All went well until Moses Reed hollered that he was stuck. Sure enough, his feet were mired in quicksand. Shields and York threw him a rope, but he sunk up to his knees before they managed to pull him out.

I have not got another deer since that first. Could it have been a lucky shot?

Sgt. Pryor and I cut down ash trees to carve into new oars. I was glad to do this to make up for my losing several.

Some men are plagued with red, swollen lumps called boils. If a boil grows too large and painful, Capt. Lewis lances it with a sharp knife and drains out the pus. Yesterday he sliced a boil on Alex Willard's backside. He said it gave out $1/2$ a pint of putrid matter. Only Capt. Lewis would have thought to measure *that*.

I am so very glad I have not got a boil.

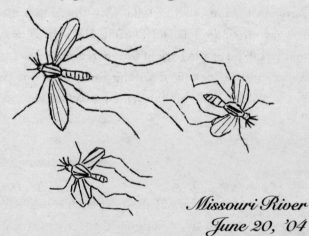

Mosquitoes swarmed thick last night. They crawled into my eyes, burrowed into my ears, trotted up my nose.

Smoke is said to keep the pests away, so I bedded down near the fire, but these mosquitoes did not mind the smoke. At last I lathered myself in stinking voyagers' grease. This discouraged them, but I don't know which is worse, mosquitoes eating me up or Seaman licking me half to death.

This evening, for fun, some men were flinging sand. Reed tossed a handful at York, and sand got in his eye. Capt. Clark flushed the eye several times with water poured through a cloth to filter it, but York says the eye still pains him. Saint Peter fashioned a patch for York to wear over the eye while it heals.

Missouri River
June 22, '04

The air smells sweet here. Wild crab apple trees bloom, as do raspberry bushes and plum trees. Herds of deer nibble young willows on the riverbank. If we get to pick our reward land in the west, I will choose this lovely spot for Ma.

Near mouth of Kansas River
June 28, '04

We are camped for a few days to repair the boats and dry our goods.

Our measuring Captain tells us that one container of Missouri River water weighs 78 pounds. The same amount of water from the Kansas River weighs only 72. The difference, he says, is mud.

York's eye is healing. He no longer needs the patch.

The Fields brothers went hunting and found an orphaned wolf pup. They say they hope to tame it. When they brought the pup to camp, Seaman circled it, growling. Reuben shouted at him to *git!* Poor Seaman slunk off into the woods. He did not come when I whistled, so I went searching for him. I found him lying with his head on his paws. He followed me back to camp, but he has not been his usual eager self tonight.

Kansas River Camp
June 29, '04

Dang! I slept so sound I missed the excitement.

We had unloaded the white pirogue to repair her hull. All the goods she carried, including the whiskey kegs, were set out on shore. Collins stood guard last night, and the sight of the kegs proved too much temptation for him. He left his post and tapped a keg. Hugh Hall, also on guard, came by and joined in the drinking. At sunup, Charlie discovered the two of them having a merry time. They tell me there was quite a ruckus when he tried to arrest them.

This morning we had another court-martial. Colter,

Newman, Gass, and Thompson served as jury. All involved in the trial put on their dress uniforms. Collins pleaded, "Not guilty!" Yet when he was tried, he was found guilty, and sentenced to one hundred lashes on his bare back. Seeing how Collins's trial went, Hall pleaded, "Guilty!" He was sentenced to fifty lashes.

We rowed awhile, then stopped to carry out the sentences. The Captains said this time all must witness the punishment. My heart sank as Collins took off his shirt and his arms were tied around a tree trunk. The poor man still had stripes on his back from his last whipping. Each member of the jury took a turn flogging Collins with a lash made of leather strips. When it came Colter's turn, he laid into Collins with all his might, as now the Expedition will be short of whiskey.

Those of us not on the jury stood by and counted out the lashes: *One! Two! Three!* At *Ten!* Collins's back was cut and bloodied. Around *Fifty!* the poor man passed out. Yet the whipping continued until we counted: *Ninety-nine! One hundred!*

I never will forget the sight of Collins's raw back. Nor the tears running down his face. Hugh Hall got his fifty lashes next. I was mighty glad when the beatings were over. Charlie, York, and I helped the whipped men down to the river. We washed their wounds and put on bandages, then got back into the boats and proceeded on, with Collins and Hall taking their places at the oars.

Seaman is still dragging around, half alive, poor dog. I hope he is not coming down sick.

Missouri River
June 30, '04

The wolf pup chewed through his rope last night and ran off.

Capt. Clark's thermometer read 96 degrees. We are all wilted by the heat, except for Seaman. He is bounding around like a frisky fool. What's got into this dog?

Missouri River
July 4, '04

We set off and made 15 miles. Capt. Lewis says we are the first Americans to travel through this new American-owned land, so we may name all that we discover. We passed a creek and named it Independence Creek in honor of the day.

When we stopped to rest, a snake bit Joseph Fields on the side of his foot. The foot quickly swelled up to the size of a small melon. Capt. Lewis checked his medicine kit and found that Dr. Rush recommends Peruvian bark for snakebite. The Captain mashed it up with lard, forming a sticky paste. He spread this paste, which he calls a poultice, on a cloth, then tied the cloth around Joseph's foot, hoping it will draw out any poison.

York says he makes snakebite poultice by chopping onions and garlic to a fine mash. Drewyer says freshly chewed tobacco put on a bite draws out the poison fast. Colter told how once he was alone in the woods when he was bit by a rattler. He slashed the bite with his knife, poured gunpowder into the wound, and set it afire. Colter rolled up his pant leg to show us the result of this treatment—a most impressive scar.

Joseph Fields is lucky that Colter is not treating his snakebite.

At close of day, Capt. Clark lit a small candle called a firing taper. He held it to the charge of the cannon. The cannon was not loaded, but it fired off a fine, loud boom to celebrate the 28th year of our nation's Independence.

***

Missouri River
July 5, '04

We expected to meet some Oto and Missouri Indians by now. So far we have seen none.

Missouri River
July 7, '04

Hot, hot day. Sweat poured off us as we rowed and we got to stinking pretty bad. Capt. Lewis says we men throw off more sweat than he thought possible to pass through a human body. (I am only grateful he does not wish to measure it.)

Midday Frazer fell down, dizzy with heatstroke. We stopped and Capt. Lewis made a deep cut into Frazer's arm to let his blood flow freely. This was done to clear his system. After a time, Frazer passed out.

York says a hat protects against heatstroke. From here on out, I will be wearing mine.

Missouri River
July 8, '04

Frazer is better, but others are sick with terrible headaches and boils. All of us are worn down. To improve our health, the Captains have appointed a Superintendent of Provision for each mess. The Super is to try to find berries, greens, and such to cook along with our meat.

And, from now on, we are to wash the cooking pots after every use.

Collins is our Super. Because of his new duty, he no longer has to stand guard, pitch tents, collect firewood, or find tree limbs for drying meat. We of his mess will take his part.

Missouri River
July 9, '04

Standing guard tonight, I spied a campfire across the river. I alerted Capt. Lewis. He ordered me to fire off some shots. I did. We waited to hear return fire, but no one fired back.

"Could be the campfire of a Teton Sioux war party," said Old Dorion.

Twice as many men as usual are now standing guard. Our rifles are loaded and ready in case of attack. The Captains say those not on guard should get some sleep to be ready for whatever lies ahead. Colter lies next to me, snoring like a bear. I wish I were so fearless.

Missouri River
July 10, '04

No attack in the night. At sunup, we boarded the boat. Keeping quiet, we crossed the river to the opposite shore, our guns cocked and ready. We snuck up to where I'd seen the campfire, and there were our own hunters, still sleeping. We woke them, and they were most surprised to see us. They said they never heard our shots.

"Must be the wind was blowing away from our camp last night," said Old Dorion.

Why did I have to spot that campfire? We got all riled up for nothing.

Missouri River
July 11, '04

A terrible thing has happened. Alex Willard was so worn out that he lay down last night while on guard duty. He is accused of falling asleep.

Capt. Lewis called us together. "The punishment for falling asleep while on guard is the same as that for a deserter," he said. "The prisoner will be shot."

Alex Willard, shot? Unthinkable! Who would carry out such a horrible punishment? I could as easily have laid down as Willard did. We are all bone tired.

Missouri River
July 12, '04

The Captains put on their dress uniforms first thing this morning and conducted Willard's trial themselves. Willard pleaded guilty to lying down, but to the charge of falling asleep, he pleaded, "Not guilty!" After the trial, when the charge of falling asleep was read out, Capt. Lewis stood and said, "Guilty."

Guilty! I felt as if I'd been punched in the stomach. I could not breathe.

Then Capt. Clark stood and said, "Willard will not be shot. He is sentenced to one hundred lashes on his bare back for four days running."

It is a terrible punishment, but Willard is grateful for it. I am, too.

Seeing how tired we are, Capt. Lewis has declared today a day of rest.

Straight off, Charlie, Whitehouse, and I went down to the river. We washed our clothes and strung them on branches to dry. We unpacked our woolens and sunned them on rocks. I stitched up what needed mending. Then we aired the jackets and shirts packed for the Indian chiefs. We unloaded the white pirogue and hauled her out of the water so Sgt. Pryor could check the patch on her hull. Any wet gunpowder we spread out on cloths in a sunny spot. We oiled and cleaned our rifles, the four blunderbusses, and the cannon. Drewyer went out and shot eight deer. I helped him clean them. We cut the meat away from the bones and sliced it up. We left some pieces large for roasting over the fire. Other pieces we cut into strips to be dried for trip rations.

We are all much improved by this day of rest.

Set off under a clear sky. Without warning, dark clouds blew over. Violent wind struck the boat so fierce that she heeled over on her side. We all leaped out and grabbed the anchor ropes. Rain and waves pounded us for some forty minutes, but we managed to keep hold of the boat. A few of Capt. Clark's journal pages blew away, and no one could save them. The storm ended as quick as it began, and the river turned smooth as glass.

Shortly after the storm, three large elk galloped along the riverbank. Drewyer shot one but only wounded it. The elk ran into the river. I scrambled back into the boat, grabbed my gun, and jumped in after it. Seaman leaped in behind me. I went after the elk, hoping to bring it in for the party, but it proved the faster swimmer. I swam back to the boat and handed my gun to Charlie. Then the dog and I splashed about in the river. At last Capt. Lewis called, "Come, puppies! Back to the boat!"

Tonight we whipped Willard for the third time. It pained me to do it, his back is so raw.

I am up early this foggy morning, my 17th birthday. I have told no one. I don't want to hear any jokes about being a pup. I only hope this next year will greatly improve me. So far on our journey I have:

lost 4 oars, 1 pole, 1 knife (found)

steered the boat too near a tree and broke the mast

shot only 1 deer

Seaman is curled beside me as I write. I should add to my list:

I have made friends with 1 dog.

Missouri River
July 16, '04

What a surprise last night! I was in the boat when suddenly Drewyer ran at me like an angry bear, swooped me up, and tossed me into the river. I thought I had been harshly discarded from the party. Then I heard men laughing, and Charlie started singing. It seems that Capt. Lewis knew my birthdate from when I signed on and arranged a celebration. After my dunking, I enjoyed a fine supper, topped by one of York's plum tarts. I did *not* hold back. Saint Peter played his fiddle then, and we danced by the fire. Drewyer sang a French song. He said it was about a girl named Marie-Claire from St. Charles. I took my first drink of whiskey. It burned my lips and throat and made me feel dizzy. What does Colter see in it?

In spite of my mighty appetite and all my many failings, the men in the Corps seem fond of their Pup. No man could ask for a better birthday.

Capt. Clark invited me to hunt with him. We climbed a hill and at the top, looked out and saw tall grass, waving in the wind. There was not a single tree, only grass as far as the eye could see. An ocean of grass. So this is the prairie.

Collins and I picked cherries from trees growing beside the river. Collins put some into the whiskey barrel. He says come a cold winter day, we will be glad he did.

Goodrich caught a big, light-colored fish here, which accounts for the name of our camp.

The Captains sent Drewyer and Saint Peter out to find some Oto. They took tobacco for a present. They are to invite the Oto chiefs to visit us. We will wait here for them to come.

Drewyer and Saint Peter returned. They found the Oto villages deserted.

I shot another deer! Collins roasted it, and it tasted fine. I am only sorry that Charlie has a bellyache and could not eat a bite of it.

After dinner, the Captains and others of us who keep journals wrote beside the fire. Then the Captains turned in, Saint Peter took up his fiddle, and we men began to dance. Only Moses Reed sat off by himself, brooding. I think he is sorry he came on the Expedition.

Drewyer was hunting and met a Missouri brave. He has brought him to our camp. With Drewyer signing, the brave told us that smallpox killed most of his people. So few are left that the Missouri have joined with the Oto as one nation. The Oto villages are deserted now because the Oto are on the plains this time of year, hunting buffalo. The brave promised to bring some chiefs to meet with us after the hunt.

Charlie's stomach still pains him. Sick as he is, he says he hopes Capt. Lewis will not try to clear his system.

***

We are camped atop high bluffs overlooking the river, waiting for the Oto chiefs. We have raised a flag to show that the United States owns this land.

Colter is trapping beaver as we go. He gives the meat to the party.

"But the pelts are mine," he says.

No one says different.

I shot a fat buck. I think I have the hang of hunting now.

Capt. Clark turned 34 today. York cooked him a birthday supper of venison, elk, and beaver tail. He made him a fancy dessert with cherries, plums, raspberries, currants, and grapes.

Charlie is still sick. While he rested in camp, he carved a peace pipe for us to smoke with the Oto. He decorated it with quills and beads. Capt. Clark says the pipe is flashy.

At dusk, several Oto approached our camp. We greeted them by firing our guns in the air and sending them presents of tobacco, roasted meats, and salt pork. In return, they sent us watermelons. They are now camped below the bluffs. The Captains have invited them to a council tomorrow at our campsite. The Oto seem friendly, but we are on our guard.

Hot and sunny. Willard and I rigged up our sail as an awning to shade the council site. We unpacked the bale of gifts marked OTO. We will give blue blankets, fancy dress coats, bright red leggings, and hats to the chiefs, and small items to the others. Next we unpacked our military uniforms and put them on. My paws must have grown some more, for my new boots pinch.

Midmorning, six Oto chiefs and some braves hiked up to our camp. They wore hide trousers but their chests were bare, as suited the heat of the day. Right off, they stopped to admire Seaman. Then, with Saint Peter translating, we learned that the main Oto chiefs are still out hunting buffalo. These six are lesser chiefs. Still, the Captains invited them to stand in the shade of the awning for a council.

We men stood in the blazing sun, decked out in our uniforms. Sgt. Ordway commanded: "Company, march!" We shouldered our guns and paraded up and down for the Oto. At last Sgt. Ordway called, "Halt! Present arms. Fire!" And we shot off our guns. When our display ended, the Oto nodded in appreciation, but in truth they must have thought us addle-headed to be wearing thick wool uniforms in the steaming heat.

Next Capt. Lewis faced the Oto and began to speak, saying, "Children! We come to you from America, a nation of seventeen great campfires. Children! Your French and Spanish fathers are gone beyond rising sun and will never return. Children! Your new father is Chief Thomas Jefferson, President of America. Children! The Oto now belong to the American family of nations. Children!"

The Captain's speech went on and on. Saint Peter translated it into Oto, making the speech twice as long. All the while, we men stood at attention. Sweat poured down my face. Every part of my skin not covered by the itchy wool got gnawed by mosquitoes.

Finally Capt. Lewis finished. An Oto chief replied with a short speech, for which I felt most deeply thankful.

Next Capt. Lewis gave the chiefs silver peace medals with President Jefferson's likeness on one side and a pair of hands clasped in friendship on the other. He gave the warriors combs. Then he made a great show of firing his air gun. Finally, the Captains and the chiefs smoked Charlie's flashy peace pipe. When the Oto left, Capt. Lewis declared it had been a most successful council.

As soon as the Oto were gone, I kicked off my boots and tore off my uniform. Every other private did the same. We all ran straight to the river and plunged in. Ahhh! How good that cool water felt.

This afternoon, we packed up and proceeded on. When we made camp, Moses Reed discovered he had left his knife at Council Bluffs. Capt. Lewis gave him leave to go back and get it.

Missouri River
Aug. 4, '04

Violent windstorm last night, with thunder and pouring rain. Many trees crashed into the river, which made for hard going today.

Reed has not come back with his knife. Some say he has deserted and run off to live with the Oto.

Missouri River
Aug. 6, '04

Reed has not returned. This morning Capt. Lewis ordered me to open his knapsack. Inside were only leaves and brush. The Captain ordered Drewyer and a party to find Reed and bring him back. He added: "If

Reed does not give up peacefully, shoot him."

Reed is the only one of us who lacks the spirit for our Adventure. Surely we will be no worse off without this man. I hope Drewyer never finds him.

Missouri River
Aug. 8, '04

We rounded a bend in the river and here came a ghostly white raft floating down the current toward us. This raft turned out to be made wholly of feathers from a flock of large white birds grooming themselves on a sandbar. Seeing us, the birds took flight. Capt. Lewis shot one so as to examine it. He says it is a pelican and asked Collins to sketch it. After that, the measuring began. By pouring water into the bag of skin below this bird's bill, Capt. Lewis discovered that it holds 5 gallons.

*Missouri River
Aug. 11, '04*

Old Dorion says we are moving out of Oto territory into Omaha territory. He says the Oto and Omaha are at war.

Charlie felt better this morning. He came ashore with the rest of the party to see the grave mound of Chief Blackbird, a famous Omaha ruler, who is said to be buried sitting astride his horse.

"Blackbird ruled the Omaha for years," Saint Peter

told us. "If any man challenged him, he slipped arsenic into his food and poisoned him."

The chief died four years back, yet his people still take food to his grave. They say even dead, he has strong powers.

Missouri River
Aug. 13, '04

We came to a large Omaha village that had been burned to the ground. Old Dorion said the villagers burned it themselves after so many of them died of smallpox. Some men killed their wives and children to save them from a slow, terrible death by disease. Then they killed themselves, hoping to meet their families in a better place hereafter.

Charlie's belly is aching again tonight. He looks so thin.

Missouri River
Aug. 15, '04

Game is scarce here, so we were glad when Goodrich and his party came into camp with a load of more than seven hundred fish.

Charlie is sicker yet. Tonight I held a bowl while he brought up vile green puke.

Missouri River
Aug. 17, '04

Capt. Lewis says Charlie is now too weak to be bled. I am so worried for him. York and I stayed up with him last night. I laid wet cloths on his head to cool his burning fever. York tried to feed him soup, but it would not stay down.

Missouri River
Aug. 18, '04

Charlie rested well last night, but he is weak and very pale. I sat beside him this morning. He talked of his ma and pa back in Kentucky.

Midmorning, I was sorry to see Drewyer lead Moses Reed into camp. Reed's hands were tied. He is a prisoner now. He kept his eyes down, not wanting to meet anyone's gaze. We will soon have another trial. If Reed is found guilty of deserting, will he be shot? I could not bear it.

Drewyer also brought along the two main Oto chiefs and some braves. He told us that in English, the chiefs' names mean something close to Big Horse and Little Thief. York quickly fixed them a meal. As the chiefs ate,

Capt. Lewis had Drewyer sign to them that they should stop sending war parties against the Omaha.

Once the chiefs were fed, the Captains held a court-martial. Reed pleaded guilty. I was relieved to hear Capt. Clark say that because he owned up to his crime, Reed would not be shot. Instead, the Captains sentenced him to run the gauntlet four times. Reed must also give up his rifle. This is a hard punishment, for all us men now feel that our guns are as much a part of us as our arms and legs. Reed is cast out of the Corps of Discovery. In the spring, he will be sent back to St. Louis in the keelboat. So, except for the whipping, Reed will get exactly what he wanted.

The Oto chiefs watched the trial with great interest, but when Drewyer told them how Reed would be punished, they begged us not to whip him. This surprised me, for Indians are often said to be warlike and savage, yet here they were, asking for mercy for our prisoner. Capt. Lewis held firm. He said Reed must be whipped for discipline to be maintained.

After the trial, each man in the party cut nine thin branches from nearby willow trees. We bundled them together in makeshift cat-o'-nine-tails. Then we formed ourselves into two lines, facing each other. Reed ran the gauntlet between us four times. Each time he passed us, we beat him with the sticks. The Oto howled for us to stop, but we kept on. Every time it came my turn, I got a sick feeling in my gut, but I whipped Reed all the same, for the sake of the Corps.

That chore being done, we set to celebrating Capt. Lewis's 30th birthday. Saint Peter fiddled, and we sang and danced beside the fire late into the night. Seaman ran in circles while we danced. The Oto chiefs watched us, nodding and smiling.

Missouri River
Aug. 19, '04

What a surprise this morning! Big Horse walked into our camp stark naked. Some braves came with him, but they were covered. Drewyer said the chief was bare to show us how poor his people are. Big Horse asked the Captains for a barrel of whiskey to take back to the young men of his tribe. It would be a gift of peace, he said, for his braves would not ride out in war parties if they had whiskey to drink at home. The Captains gave him tobacco, face paint, and beads, but no whiskey.

When Capt. Lewis began his air-gun show, I quietly went to Drewyer. I asked him to ask the Oto braves if they had any medicine for a bad stomach. None of Capt. Lewis's herbs or pills have helped Charlie, but I thought the Oto might have a cure. Drewyer signed to a brave he called Iron Eyes about the medicine. Iron Eyes listened. Then he took off his necklace made of beads, feathers, and porcupine quills. From it dangled a small leather pouch. Drewyer said it is a medicine bundle. Iron Eyes handed me the necklace. This was not the sort of medicine I had in mind, but I took it. I could think of no better way to thank him, so I gave him my tomahawk.

After the Oto left, I went to where Charlie lay. I showed him the Oto necklace. I told him that it was strong medicine and would help to make him well. Charlie is fevered and in terrible pain, but he smiled as I slipped the necklace over his head.

Missouri River
Aug. 20, '04

Capt. Clark, York, and I sat up with Charlie through the night. I have never seen a man more miserable. This morning we carried him onto the boat and set off, but Charlie was so ill that Capt. Lewis ordered us to pull ashore at a spot sheltered from the wind where we could build a fire. We have water warming now to make a bath for Charlie. We hope this will rouse him.

I have lost my friend. As he lay on the riverbank, Charlie reached for my hand. "I am going away," he said, his voice so weak I could hardly hear him. "I want you to write a letter for me." I readied my quill to take down his words, but before he could say anything more, Charlie passed away.

Oh, Charlie, you were like a brother to me.

Cannot write more now.

We dressed Charlie in his uniform and laid him in a wooden coffin, built by Gass and Sgt. Pryor. We all put on our dress uniforms and carried Charlie up to the knob of a hill that overlooks the river. There we dug his grave and lowered him into it. Capt. Lewis read the funeral service. I spoke up, saying, "Charles Floyd died with great dignity at only 22 years of age. He was a fine sergeant and a leader of men on this Expedition." Others murmured, "Amen." We marked Charlie's grave with a red cedar post, which Whitehouse had branded to say:

C. Floyd, Sergeant
1st United States Regiment, Infantry,
1782–1804

With heavy hearts we left Charlie there on that hill, and we proceeded on.

Mouth of Floyd's River
Aug. 22, '04

As we went, we named a creek flowing into the Missouri Charles Floyd's Creek. We named the bluffs above it Charles Floyd's Bluffs. We are camped beside the mouth of a wide river now called Charles Floyd's River. I believe all this naming would have pleased Charlie.

By the fire tonight, the Captains gave Charlie's things to his cousin, Sgt. Pryor. He says when the keelboat goes down the river next spring, he will send Charlie's shot pouch and the Oto necklace back to his folks in Kentucky.

After the fire died down, Sgt. Pryor found me. He gave me Charlie's tomahawk. He said he thought Charlie would like for me to have it. I had to get up and walk some after that. It hurts me to think I will never again see Charlie's face.

Or Pa's face either.

I set out hunting with Joseph Fields. We are camped for the night on the prairie.

Missouri River
Aug. 23, '04

Woke up in a sandstorm. All we could do was lie back down with our eyes shut and wait for the wind to die down. When at last it did, every tree and blade of grass as far as we could see was coated with fine grains of sand. We were also well coated.

I had never seen a buffalo. This afternoon I was treated to the sight of more of them than I could count. They are huge, majestic creatures. Joseph shot one. It was so big that I had to run to the riverbank and shout for assistance. Ten men came to help us butcher the buffalo and carry the meat back to the boat.

(buffalo)

We dined on buffalo steak, tongue, and hump. It was a fine supper, and no one held back.

Afterward we voted for a sergeant to take Charlie's place. The carpenter Patrick Gass won the election with nineteen votes.

Missouri River
Aug. 24, '04

"We are traveling through Sioux territory," Capt. Lewis warns us time and again. "Be ever on your guard!"

The soil here is rich in minerals. Capt. Lewis has identified brass, copper, and cobalt by tasting small amounts of each. All went well until he tasted a mineral that made his stomach cramp. He quickly dosed himself with Thunder Clappers and went off into the woods for a spell. He came back feeling better. He now believes he has identified arsenic.

Above Vermillion River
Aug. 25, '04

The Omaha and Oto call a nearby rise Hill of the Little Devils. They say humanlike devils only 18 inches tall, but with very large heads, live inside this hill. They claim that these devils shoot poison-tipped arrows at anyone who comes near. Three Omaha braves were recently found slain on this hill, and nothing will persuade the native people to go near it.

I was most eager to climb this Devil Hill, as was every man in our party, but the Captains chose only ten men to go. Even the dog was invited. I was not.

Instead, I joined a party of hunters. Reuben Fields brought down five deer. I shot my first elk. This made me feel some better about missing the Little Devils. When we stopped to jerk the meat, the horses strayed, so we had to carry the game to the boat on our backs. Then Drewyer and I went to look for the horses. We quickly found Lizzy, but search as we might, we have not yet found Mary Jane. We are camped in the woods and will search for her tomorrow.

Mosquitoes very troublesome.

Above Vermillion River
Aug. 26, '04

Vermillion means bright red, and red is what this river is. It gets its color from the red clay along its banks.

Drewyer and I decided to split up to look for Mary Jane. We drew sticks to see who would ride. Drewyer got the short stick, so he took off on foot while I rode Lizzy. After some hours, I spotted hoof tracks. I followed them and found Mary Jane, grazing on prairie grass. Leading her behind, I rode to the meeting place Drewyer and I had agreed upon. Drewyer wasn't there. I hollered for him in every direction, but he never hollered back. He will come soon.

Drewyer has not come. I figure I'd best stay put so he will know where to find me. I have tethered the horses and made a fire. A chill is on the air. I did not expect to be gone long, so brought no camping gear. At least I have my possible bag.

Night: I am alone in Sioux territory.

Woods
Aug. 27, '04

Woke at dawn. No Drewyer. I hope he has not run into any Sioux.

Mary Jane looks sickly. I will tether her so she can graze while I go hunt for Drewyer.

Rode Lizzy out from the camp. I called Drewyer's name again and again. I fired many shots. No answer. Late afternoon, I came back to the meeting place. Mary Jane was still here, but Drewyer was not. Can those Little Devils have got him?

Shot a rabbit. Dined on roasted rabbit, juicy plums, and grapes. As I ate, I figured that if he could,

Drewyer would have gone back to the boat. At day-break, I will, too.

Hard wind last night. Rose at dawn. Fine breakfast of plums and grapes. Buried my campfire and rode Lizzy toward the river, leading Mary Jane behind. Kept an ear cocked for shots fired by a hunting party but heard not a one. At noon, climbed up a high bluff and looked down on a wide stretch of river. No boat.

Another rabbit for supper. Ate alone beside my small fire. I think of Charlie. I miss him terrible. I miss Seaman's eager face. I miss Collins's suppers. And the men joking and laughing by the cook fires. I long to hear Saint Peter's fiddle. To see Colter, York, and the Fields brothers stomping to its lively tunes. The only tunes I hear are sung by wolves, howling at the moon. And by mosquitoes, buzzing as they try to eat me for supper.

Bad storm last night. The thunder put me in a mind of Capt. Lewis's Thunder Clappers, and I had myself a little laugh. When the rain let up, I was glad for the tinderbox in my possible bag. Got a fire going. Fed it on wet sticks, which made it sizzle.

This morning, I emptied out my shot pouch and counted my bullets. Only three left! I thought I had a dozen. These will last me until I catch up to the boat. I can make 15 to 20 miles a day on horseback, so I will catch it soon.

Plums and grapes for breakfast. Now to get Mary Jane and Lizzy and ride down to the river, where I am sure to find my Corps.

Rode a great distance beside the river. No boat.

Woods
Aug. 30, '04

Thick fog this morning. Forced down plums and grapes. The taste of them is bitter to me now. No matter how many I eat, they never fill me up.

Hard riding through the thick brush beside the river. Headed inland to the prairie, where I can make better time. Came upon a gang of buffalo. I thought it a good use of my bullets to try to get one, for this would mean the end of my hunger—no more cursed grapes! And I could take meat back to the Corps. Three times I loaded my gun, took aim, and fired, but no buffalo lost its life this day on my account.

That was the last of my bullets.

Came upon several sets of footprints by the river this afternoon. My heart leaped up at this human sign, the first I have seen in five days. I figured them for the prints of men Capt. Lewis sent to find me, and followed them until the light gave out. I called the names of those most likely to be in a search party—"Drewyer! Colter! Shields! Fields! Bratton! Gibson! Seaman!" No one answered—nor even barked.

Tomorrow I will find them.

Woods
Aug. 31, '04

Up at first light to follow the tracks.

Followed the footprints to the prairie, where I lost them. Most likely the prints were made by a party of Sioux. Do they know I am here? Are they watching me? If they find me, what will they do?

Spent this afternoon whittling sticks into bullet shapes, rounded at one end, sharpened at the other. I cannot shoot one as a trial. I have no powder to waste. But I plan to fire a wooden bullet into the heart of the next rabbit or deer unlucky enough to cross my path.

In the meantime, grapes and plums, plums and grapes.

***

Woods
Sept. 1, '04

Gone from the party for a week now. Can Capt. Lewis think that I deserted? If he opens my pack, he will find my blanket, my extra shirt and breeches, the rest of my bullets and powder. Surely the Captain knows this pup would never desert him.

I sit by my fire, thinking back to how Charlie and I made a batch of Capt. Lewis's portable soup. How we thought it tasted like mud. (I would gladly eat it now!) How we made up words to go with Saint Peter's fiddle tunes. How we danced with those French girls back in St. Charles. How I miss Charlie.

Woods and more woods
Sept. 2, '04

Bad storm last night. A whole batch of wild turkeys ran through the woods this morning. Tried to shoot them with my wooden bullets, but they ran too fast.

I talk to Mary Jane and Lizzy as we go. They are my only companions. Mary Jane barely nibbles at the grass now. She is so thin I can count her ribs.

Woods
Sept. 3, '04

Mary Jane gave out and died this day, and I am very sorry.

Success! I shot a rabbit! I quickly skinned it, cut the meat into chunks and threaded them onto a stick. My hands shook so, I could hardly hold the flints to make a fire, but at last I got one going. The smell of meat roasting was too much for me, and I gobbled down the first piece raw, barely warm. Now, with meat in my belly, my spirits are much improved.

Whittled dozens of wooden bullets and went hunting. Turkeys, rabbits, even deer scampered by me all day. They seemed to taunt me, daring me to shoot them. I shot, but never hit a one. My powder supply is very low. My guts are cramping up from all the grapes and plums.

Night: Awakened by a rustling in the brush. I saw a large shape standing over me. I jumped up shouting, "Drewyer! Drewyer!" only to find myself face-to-face with a bear. I must have scared him good, leaping up and shouting the way I did. That bear let out a scream, turned tail, and raced back into the woods. I do not think he will be back.

***

Alone.

Weak with hunger. Too weak to travel. Camped beside a stream last night. Whittled a stick to a point and tried to gig a fish. No luck.

I will stay here. The stream has fresh drinking water. I can keep an eye on the river.

I wrap myself in the saddle blankets, yet the cold seeps through. I hear screams of small animals as they are caught by owls. And always the wolves, howling.

Sixteen days missing from the party. Capt. Lewis must think me dead. I feel half dead, on this purple diet, fit for a songbird but not for a man.

I wonder who sits next to Whitehouse in the keelboat, pulling at my oar?

I have given up all hope of finding the boat. My dreams

of an Adventure are ended. I will earn no western land for my family. Ma, should this journal come back to you one day, please know I am so very sorry. You were counting on me, and I have let you down.

I am trembling from lack of food. Desperate men eat their horses to keep from starving, I know that, but old Lizzy has been my only friend all these days in the wilderness, and I will starve before I eat her.

I sit now at the river's edge in the pouring rain, my one poor horse shivering beside me. We will wait here. Maybe some French trappers will paddle down the river and come to our rescue.

Missouri River
Sept. 12, '04

I sat in the rain beside the river all morning. I felt lower than ever in my life. Around midday, I thought I heard a dog barking. I looked around. The woods were empty. No trappers' boat floated down the river. I feared that my starving condition was causing me to hear imaginary noises. Then my eye caught sight of a boat coming *up* the river. A boat I never thought to lay my eyes on again: the keelboat of the CORPS OF DISCOVERY!

My knees were so weak, I could barely stand to wave at this mirage, for so I thought it had to be. Never in all the time I wandered did I suspect that I might have got *ahead* of the boat!

Seaman leaped overboard and swam toward me. I heard Capt. Lewis call him back, not understanding what the dog was about. Then Saint Peter spotted me and gave a holler. The boat turned toward the shore.

Seaman bounded out of the river, ran, and leaped into my arms, knocking me to the ground, just as he had when first we met. River water streamed off his fur as he licked my face with his wide pink tongue. I have never been so glad of a bath!

The boat pulled ashore. The crew put their arms around me, one after the other, and I wept for my good fortune. When Drewyer's turn came, he gave me a great bear hug, nearly crushing what was left of me. He said he'd followed hoofprints for two days, thinking they were Mary Jane's, only to come upon a strayed Indian pony in the prairie. By that time he figured I'd have gone back to the boat, so went back himself.

Capt. Lewis gave me a small amount of jerked meat and some whiskey. He asked to hear my tale. I told how for sixteen days I chased after the boat, thinking it was ahead. And how, for twelve of those days, I was without bullets.

Capt. Clark put an arm around my shoulder and said, "So you near to starved to death in this land of plenty."

"A starved Pup is likely to eat even *more* than before," Capt. Lewis added, "if such a thing is possible."

He said it with a smile, and I knew my Captain was glad to have me back.

I was relieved of duties this day to gather my strength. But the current was swift, and when the boat nearly capsized and a dozen men plunged into the river to hold her fast, I plunged right in with them. No amount of hard labor nor icy water can make me lose my good spirits.

Whooo-eee! I am back with my Corps!

Missouri River
Sept. 13, '04

I missed the meeting with the Yankton Sioux. Drewyer told me they were friendly. Their chiefs have agreed to travel to Washington to meet President Jefferson. The Captains asked Old Dorion to stay behind and escort them on the trip.

Last night we camped near a village of animals the Frenchmen call little dogs. They look like plump, golden squirrels without tails and live community style in a maze of tunnels under the ground. By pouring gallons and gallons of water down a hole, Capt. Lewis managed to flush out one little dog and capture it. The Fields brothers made it a cage and are looking after it. Come spring, Capt. Lewis plans to send the little dog to the President.

***

Hard rain last night. Set off early. We passed the creek I had camped beside for several days. The Captains say they will name it Shannon's Creek, but I had rather do without this honor.

Great clouds of smoke rose from the prairie tonight. Drewyer says this blaze was likely set by Teton Sioux scouts to warn their people that white men are approaching.

Capt. Clark issued each man a red flannel shirt for the coming winter. I was mighty glad, for when we stopped yesterday and unpacked our provisions to air them out, I found my extra shirt and trousers had rotted from the damp. That left me with only the clothes on my back.

Capt. Lewis took six of us out on a ramble. We stopped by a village of the little dogs. We sat awhile and watched them pop in and out of their holes, always seeming in a great hurry. The Captain saw a rattlesnake slithering away from their village and shot it. He slit it open with his knife and found the snake had swallowed a little dog whole. Hawks circled overhead. We believe they make meals of the little dogs, too. We saw wild goats, porcupines, hares, and polecats. Walking farther onto the prairie, we were amazed at the sight of buffalo in numbers too large even for Capt. Lewis to count. We ate the dinner we had brought while watching herds of elk and antelope graze. Not far from these herds were restless packs of coyotes and wolves, scouting for their dinner. I saw more animals in this one day than in all the other days of my life put together.

We have plenty of meat, so we shot no game.

Big Bend
Sept. 21, '04

We camped last night on a sandbar. Some time after midnight, Sgt. Pryor blew his horn for an alarm. We jumped up and cocked our guns, ready for a Teton Sioux attack, but Sgt. Pryor yelled that the sand beneath our boat was giving way. Instantly we tossed our bedrolls into the boat, piled in, and took off. We were hardly away when our campsite was sucked down into the river and disappeared. All this was visible due to the light of the full moon.

***

Missouri River
1,283 miles from Fort Wood River
Sept. 23, '04

Three Indian boys swam across the river to our campsite this evening. Drewyer signed with them, and I was able to understand some of what was said. The boys were Teton Sioux. They said two large Teton villages lie north of here. Capt. Lewis gave the boys twists of tobacco. Through Drewyer, he told them to give them to their chiefs and to ask them to come to council with us. The boys agreed to do so and swam back across the river.

At last we will meet the mighty Tetons.

Capt. Lewis gathered us together. "President Jefferson most desperately wishes us to befriend the Teton Sioux," he said. "This is a vital part of our mission. We must let nothing get in the way of our becoming friends with this powerful nation. Nothing! Those of you keeping journals, write down all you can of our council with the Tetons. We must record this important event for posterity!"

The Captain is more anxious than I have ever seen him.

Bad River, Teton territory
Sept. 24, '04

As we paddled toward the Teton villages, Colter ran up the bank, yelling, "The Tetons stole Lizzy!"

We pulled ashore. Five Tetons appeared.

Capt. Clark said, "Our horse has been stolen."

Saint Peter translated this into Omaha. According to Saint Peter, the Tetons replied that if their warriors took the horse, they will return it.

We made camp on the bank of what the Tetons call Bad River.

"Unpack the bale of gifts for the Tetons, Pup," Capt. Lewis said. "And you'd better unpack one of the extra bales, too. I have a feeling we are going to need a large quantity of gifts."

Two Tetons led Lizzy into our camp this afternoon.

"No more need be said about this," said Capt. Clark.

But Colter muttered, "A stolen horse is a bad omen."

Bad Humored Island
Sept. 25, '04

We set up for council on a sandbar at the mouth of the Bad River. Whitehouse and I dug a hole, planted a flagstaff, and raised our American flag. We set up the sail for an awning and readied the gifts. I was putting on my uniform when I noticed many Tetons gathering on both sides of the river. The men are armed with bows and arrows. We are badly outnumbered. What will happen?

Hundreds of Tetons are lining the riverbanks. More come by the minute! We are still waiting for their chiefs to come.

Warriors are paddling two chiefs out to the sandbar. Four women are in the boats as well. Our meeting with the Tetons is about to begin.

The women with the Tetons were Omaha prisoners, lately captured in battle. The chiefs had heard that one of our party speaks Omaha, so they brought the prisoners to help translate. Saint Peter spoke with them. He says that in English, the chiefs are called Black Buffalo and Partisan.

The Captains brought out Charlie's flashy peace pipe and smoked with the Tetons. (How this would have pleased Charlie!)

Then Capt. Lewis began his speech: "Children! We come to you from America, a nation of seventeen great campfires!" Saint Peter gave Capt. Lewis's words to the prisoners in Omaha. The prisoners gave it to the Tetons in the Sioux tongue. Yet before long, everyone started talking at once. Drewyer stepped in. He tried to translate using hand signs, but Capt. Lewis cut him off, saying the signs fell short of giving the true meaning of his speech. I was sorry that Old Dorion was not here, as he speaks first-rate Sioux.

The Captain signaled for us to begin parading. We did so, holding high a U.S. flag. Then we fired off a round of shots. Next came the presents. Capt. Lewis seemed to think that Black Buffalo was the main chief, for he gave him a big peace medal, a red coat, leggings, and a three-cornered hat. He gave Partisan lesser gifts. Partisan scowled and said we must give him the red pirogue and everything in it. At least we think this is what he said, but not having a proper interpreter, we cannot be sure.

To change the subject, Capt. Lewis invited the chiefs and some warriors to come aboard the keelboat. The Tetons stepped into the white pirogue. I helped row them out to our boat. From my seat in the pirogue, I watched Capt. Lewis pour each chief a drink of whiskey. After a few swallows, Partisan began to stumble around, giving a great show of being drunk. The Tetons on the riverbank cheered him, enjoying the show. Capt. Clark said it was time for the chiefs to go, but they did not seem eager to return to shore. Partisan kept up his act. Finally Capt. Lewis motioned to us rowers, and we boarded the keelboat. By taking hold of Partisan, we managed to get him back into the pirogue. The other Tetons followed. Capt. Clark got in, too, and we began rowing toward the shore.

How glad I was to get those Tetons back to land! Yet more trouble lay ahead. Three warriors ran to the pirogue and grabbed our bowline. Another threw his arms around our mast. Partisan swaggered up to Capt. Clark. He began talking and gesturing, and we needed no translator to know the meaning of his words. He said our party could not go on.

The Tetons on shore fell silent, waiting to see what Capt. Clark would do.

We men of the Corps waited, too.

Capt. Clark grew red in the face. He drew his sword. He called to Capt. Lewis on the keelboat, "Prepare for action!"

Capt. Lewis called to the men on board, "Load the cannon!"

Capt. Clark ordered us men in the pirogue to ready our arms. My fingers shook so, I could hardly cock my gun.

On shore, the hundreds of Teton warriors strung their bows. They quickly pulled arrows from their quivers and fitted them to their bowstrings.

The men on the keelboat put up the locker lids as shields.

Everyone was ready for a terrible battle.

Then Black Buffalo stepped forward. He yanked our bowline away from his warriors. Holding the rope, Black Buffalo spoke. Saint Peter told us that he said he might let us go on, but his men could easily follow us and kill us any time they pleased.

Capt. Clark's face grew redder still. "If anything happens to us," he told Black Buffalo, "Chief Jefferson will send mighty warriors to destroy the Teton Sioux."

I could not breathe. I thought my chest would burst. A battle seemed sure to start.

Black Buffalo spoke again. And when Saint Peter

told Capt. Clark what he had said, the Captain had Saint Peter tell him a second time to make sure he understood. For in the midst of this tense standoff, Black Buffalo had asked whether some Teton women and children from his own village up the river might come aboard the keelboat to see its many wonders. Capt. Clark smiled and agreed that they might. Black Buffalo dropped our bow rope. We lowered our rifles. The warriors slid their arrows back into their quivers. Once more, Black Buffalo had found a way to end the trouble.

Capt. Clark climbed back into the white pirogue. We started rowing for the keelboat. We had not gone far when Black Buffalo waded into the river, calling out that he wished to spend the night on our boat. Capt. Clark muttered under his breath but ordered us to turn around. We rowed back to shore and picked up Black Buffalo and his men.

Once they were aboard the keelboat, we rowed a mile upstream. We dropped anchor by a willow island, where we are camped for the night. Capt. Clark named it Bad Humored Island, as this describes our state of mind.

Northern Teton village
Sept. 26, '04

Black Buffalo and his men stayed with us all night. No one slept much.

We set off early. Hundreds of Tetons lined the shore. They kept their eyes on us as we headed upriver toward Black Buffalo's village. The chief, all friendly now, showed us where to anchor our boat to make it easy for women and children to come aboard. Capt. Clark and some of us men stayed on the boat to receive the visitors. Capt. Lewis led a party to the village.

Three hours passed. Capt. Clark grew uneasy. He sent Sgt. Gass to the village to check on Capt. Lewis, and Sgt. Gass returned, saying all was well. The people of the village were preparing a great feast and a dance in our honor. They invited Capt. Clark and more men to come to the village. I hope I am picked to go.

Whitehouse and I went with Capt. Clark to Black Buffalo's village. As we drew near, we smelled the good scent of roasting buffalo. The Tetons live in houses, called lodges, made of stretched buffalo hides painted red or white. Each lodge has a tall pole at its center. Whitehouse has made a study of the Missouri River nomads. He told me that a lodge can easily be taken down, rolled around its pole, and dragged to a new spot by a dog.

Late in the afternoon, the Tetons led us to a large Council Lodge. Braves spread a white buffalo robe on the ground. They motioned for Capt. Clark to sit on the robe. He did, and eight braves picked it up and carried him into the Council Lodge. We men followed. Dozens of elders and warriors sat in a circle inside. Some wore hawks' feathers braided into their hair. The braves set Capt. Clark down next to Black Buffalo. Whitehouse and I sat down behind a row of Tetons. Soon after, other braves carried Capt. Lewis into the lodge on a buffalo robe. They set him down on the other side of the chief. Now it was Black Buffalo's turn to show off for our party.

The chief chanted what sounded like a prayer, then lit a pipe. He passed it around the circle, and we all smoked in turn. My throat burned, but I managed not to cough.

Capt. Clark rose to his feet. With Saint Peter translating, he asked Black Buffalo, as a gesture of peace, to let the Omaha prisoners go free. Black Buffalo's only answer was to order the feast to begin. I have never tasted better than that roasted buffalo. The Tetons also served what, for them, is a great delicacy—roasted dog. Whitehouse ate some so as not to offend our hosts, but I could not bring myself to touch it. Capt. Clark also passed it up.

Night came on. A fire was lit in the center of the lodge. Warriors danced in, decked out in face paint, porcupine quills, and feathers. They sang, beat drums, and jangled sticks topped with deer-hoof rattles. They took turns leaping into the circle and singing. Next, Teton women danced into the lodge, singing and waving scalps. It was a chilling sight, that scalp dance, and no doubt meant to frighten us, but our Captains cheered and tossed twists of tobacco and beads to the dancers. We men did the same. The festivities kept up till way past midnight.

When the dance ended, Black Buffalo invited us to stay in his village, but the Captains said no. We returned to our boat.

Late: I was in the cabin talking to Capt. Lewis when Saint Peter knocked. He rushed in, saying that he had just come from visiting the Omaha prisoners and they told him that tomorrow the Tetons plan to attack us. Capt. Lewis hurried from the cabin. He doubled the number of men standing guard. Here we go, another sleepless night.

Northern Teton village
Sept. 27, '04

We have been on high alert this morning, expecting trouble. Yet no man wants to stay on the boat all day and miss whatever excitement might happen, so we take turns paddling to the village. At last Colter and I got to go. In the village, we got separated. When it came time for us to leave, Colter appeared grinning and wearing a fine hawk-feather hair ornament.

I had guard duty tonight, so I stayed on the keelboat with the other guards while both Captains and a party of men went into the village for another scalp dance. Around midnight, I caught sight of the first batch of men paddling back to the boat in the white pirogue. The night was very dark, but I made out Capt. Clark and Partisan sitting in the bow and Willard steering. The current was swift, and the men were having a hard time rowing. As they drew near, Willard lost control of the tiller. The current swung the pirogue around, slammed her into the keelboat, and cut right through our anchor rope. We started drifting!

Capt. Clark stood up in the pirogue and shouted, "All hands on the keelboat! Up and at the oars!"

We guards left our posts, ran to the benches, and started rowing. We tried to turn the bow into the current.

All the shouting must have alarmed Partisan, for he started shouting, too.

Then Drewyer called out that Partisan was yelling, "The Omaha are attacking!"

The riverbank quickly filled with Teton warriors. They strung their bows.

Capt. Clark shouted, "Men, ready your rifles!"

We dropped our oars. We picked up our guns and cocked them. Our boat began drifting sideways to the current. No one knew what was happening.

Capt. Clark called to the translators: "What are the Tetons saying?"

"The Omaha are attacking us!" Drewyer shouted. "The Tetons will fight them!"

"No!" cried Saint Peter. "The Tetons are attacking us! Just as the Omaha warned!"

Back and forth they went. We were more confused than ever.

At last Capt. Clark shouted, "Quiet!"

All was still. The Teton arrows were ready to fly. I took aim at a warrior on the riverbank. But could I pull the trigger?

The silence continued. Then, all at the same time, everyone understood that there were no Omaha. The Tetons lowered their bows. I lowered my rifle. We had "jumped the gun." Once more, not having a decent interpreter had brought us to the brink of war.

The Tetons left the shore. We men started rowing again, trying to turn the keelboat. Only then did I feel my feet sloshing in water. Our boat was leaking!

Sgt. Pryor called to Capt. Clark, "She's got a hole where the pirogue hit her, sir!"

I kept rowing. Others bailed. At last Sgt. Gass and Sgt. Pryor corked the hole. We rowed to the nearest island. We had lost our anchor, so we tied up to a tree. More than the usual number are standing guard tonight. Time for my watch.

Northern Teton village
Sept. 28, '04

Searched for our anchor all morning but never found it.

At last Capt. Clark said we must move on. The poor man looks worn down.

More trouble with the Tetons! As we hoisted our sail, a slew of Teton braves appeared on the riverbank. I thought they had come to see us off. Then, to my horror, I saw that all were armed with bows and arrows, spears, cutlasses, and rifles.

We lowered the sail. Braves rowed Black Buffalo and Partisan out to the keelboat. As the chiefs called to us from their boat, asking for tobacco and gifts, their warriors took hold of our bow rope and tied us up to the tree. Once more our party was held hostage by the Teton Sioux.

Capt. Clark picked up the firing taper. He lit it and held it above the loaded cannon. He told Black Buffalo to prove that he was a leader by telling his men to drop the rope.

Black Buffalo did nothing.

Capt. Lewis muttered about river pirates. Then he drew himself up and told Black Buffalo that he would give the men holding our rope one twist of tobacco— only one!—then they must let go. Capt. Lewis tossed tobacco onto the shore. Black Buffalo called to his men, and they untied our bow rope. Willard and Colter quickly hoisted our sail. We all heaved hard at our oars, out-doing any past speed record as we set off from that village.

Tonight I found Capt. Lewis standing on the deck of the keelboat, staring out at the river. "Things did not go well between us and the Teton Sioux, Pup," he said. "President Jefferson will not be pleased." He sighed then, and added, "But President Jefferson has never met any Teton Sioux."

Missouri River
Sept. 30, '04

Black Buffalo is back. No one invited him, but his men rowed him out to us and he came aboard. Saint Peter says as he understands it, the chief plans to travel with us for a stretch.

Black Buffalo is gone for good. This afternoon, the stern of the keelboat got stuck on a snag, and we wheeled around. The wind and waves were high. The boat rocked badly. We tried to push it off the snag with our poles, but we stayed stuck. So Drewyer hoisted our sail. The hard wind filled it and yanked us off the snag. Once free, the wind took us racing over the water. We men cheered and hollered to be moving at such speed, but Black Buffalo held tightly to the gunnels. When at last we slowed down, he said our boat was bad medicine and asked to be put ashore. We quickly pulled over. We gave Black Buffalo a blanket, tobacco, and a knife. He set off on foot to return to his band.

We set off upriver, putting 24 miles between us and the Teton Sioux.

Missouri River
Oct. 2, '04

The Captains warn us that the Sioux may make a surprise attack. Each time we come to a bend in the river and cannot see what lies ahead, we take up our arms.

The day passed without trouble, yet we are all worn down from expecting it.

White Goat Creek
Oct. 5, '04

Frost this morning. When Seaman barked, his warm breath made a white cloud in the air. We are cold, but no one complains, for frost means no more mosquitoes!

A herd of white goats swam by. We shot four of them, and Collins made us a tasty stew.

Missouri River
Oct. 8, '04

Dropped anchor by an Arikara village. Many Arikara came down to the river to see us. They wore handsome beaded headbands and leggings.

115

With them was a French trader, Mr. Gravelines, who came aboard. He speaks English and told us he has lived among these people for thirteen years. Not long ago, he said, tens of thousands of Arikara lived in eighteen large villages, but so many fell sick and died from smallpox that only three small villages are left. He told us the Arikara are now at war with the Mandan.

The Captains asked Mr. Gravelines to translate our talks with the Arikara, and he has agreed. This should keep us from having such problems as we had with the Teton Sioux.

Arikara council
Oct. 9, '04

We made camp across the river from an Arikara village. This morning the wind blew like fury, whipping up the sand, which stung our eyes so that we could hardly see. Yet here came the Arikara paddling over the river to council with us. They came in bull boats, made from a single bull buffalo hide stretched over a bowl-shaped willow frame. Each bull boat held five or six men, with three women paddling. When the Arikara came ashore and we stood together for council, the wind blew too hard for our words to be heard, so the women paddled their men home again.

***

The weather cleared and the Arikara came back. With
Mr. Gravelines translating, Capt. Lewis gave his
"Children!" speech. Then he gave gifts, many more
than he had offered to the Tetons. After the Captain
fired off the cannon and his air gun, he let me show off
Seaman's tricks. I believe the dog impressed these people far more than the guns.

Next, the Captains offered whiskey, but the Arikara
refused it. Later, Mr. Gravelines told us that they were
surprised we wanted to give them liquor, as it would
make them act foolish. The council ended with Chief
Man Wolf and two other chiefs shaking hands with our
Captains.

I went with the party to visit an Arikara village. York
came along. The Arikara had never seen a dark-skinned
man before, and they marveled over him. They are in

awe of his great size. They believe his dark skin is a sign of a strong spirit.

In the village, Collins put York up to some fun. York pretended to be a wild animal. He roared and chased some Arikara children, who ran from him, shrieking in delight. Capt. Clark did not like this game and quickly ended it. Later Saint Peter told me the Arikara call York the Big Medicine.

The Arikara live in domed houses made of earth, with a smoke hole at the top. The women gave us squash, corn, and beans. Saint Peter told me they dig up the beans from the winter stores of mice, but they leave other food in place of what they take so the mice will not go hungry.

When we got back to the boat, I saw that Colter was wearing a beaded antelope-skin headband and a pair of beaded leggings. He said he paid one beaver pelt for these items.

It is a great relief to be among the friendly Arikara after our hard time with the Teton Sioux.

Missouri River
Oct. 12, '04

The generous Arikara gave us a dozen bushels of corn and beans to send us on our way. We set off with great fanfare, fiddles playing and horns blowing.

We are headed for the Mandan villages. Chief

Man Wolf is traveling with us. The Captains hope he can help to make peace between the Arikara and the Mandan.

Missouri River
Oct. 13, '04

Last night after the Captains retired to the boat, we men sat around the fire. I was stitching new moccasins. Moses Reed gave John Newman the elbow.

Newman leaned forward. "I heard the Captains talking together," he whispered.

We all bent close to hear more.

"They said a Teton Sioux party is following us," Newman went on. "They expect an attack at any minute, but they don't dare tell us, for fear we will desert them."

I blurted out, "That is a lie!"

"I heard them say it," Newman said. "If we don't take action soon, the Teton squaws will be waving the tops of *our* heads in their scalp dance."

Reed spoke up: "If we follow the Captains, none of us will live to tell about it."

"We can take a pirogue and go tonight," Newman said. "Who is coming with us?"

I jumped up, shouting, "No one!" I lunged for Newman. Whitehouse did the same. Sgt. Pryor and Sgt. Gass scrambled to their feet and grabbed Reed. We held them while Sgt. Ordway went to fetch the Captains. When they heard what the two had said, Reed and Newman were bound as prisoners.

Reed cannot be punished further, but Newman is charged with mutiny. He pleaded, "Not guilty." So it was put to a jury.

We halted at noon today and held a court-martial. For the first time, I was on the jury. Collins was, too. He told me he much prefers it to being the prisoner.

We found Newman guilty as charged. His sentence of seventy-five lashes will be carried out tomorrow. Newman must also give up his gun, as Reed had to do. From here on out, he will row in the Frenchmen's pirogue. Come spring, he will also be sent back to St. Louis.

I felt sorry for Reed when he deserted, but I no longer feel sorry for him or Newman. For telling such stretchers, they deserve to miss out on this great Adventure.

Missouri River
Oct. 14, '04

Rainy morning. At noon we stopped at a sandbar. Newman stripped off his shirt. As we whipped him, Man Wolf began to cry. The punishment was halted while Capt. Clark explained to him that we had to set an example. Man Wolf agreed that setting an example was important. He said his people set an example by putting a man to death, but they never whipped anyone, ever.

Whitehouse, Colter, and I went on a ramble with Mr. Gravelines. Buffalo stretched across the prairie as far as we could see. Mr. Gravelines led us to a large tree standing alone on the prairie. He told us that the Mandan hold this tree sacred. Young men journey here. They pierce the skin of their chests and run a leather thong through the pierced holes. Then they tie the thong to this tree. They stay tied to the tree as long as they can bear it and, in this way, become brave. I stood silent, as did all the men, respectful of this tree and of these Mandan braves.

The icy rains have given Capt. Clark a stiff neck. Once again he is wrapped up in red flannel. This same freezing weather did not seem to bother a party of Teton Sioux horsemen. They galloped by us today dressed only in leather leggings, their chests bare.

***

Missouri River
Oct. 24, '04

With a light snow falling, we went hunting on a large island and met a party of Mandan. It was led by Chief Big White, so called because of his large size and light skin. With Mr. Gravelines's help, Capt. Lewis introduced Man Wolf to Big White. He said he is counting on them to make peace between their nations.

Mandan villages
Oct. 25, '04

We had to pull our boat with ropes the last stretch to the Mandan villages. As we towed, many Mandan came to see us and called out in a most friendly way. We waved to them. Yet we are on guard. Man Wolf warns us not to trust the Mandan.

Mandan campsite
1,610 miles by river from Fort Wood River
Oct. 26, '04

We are camped in a cornfield south of Big White's village. We have raised our flag.

Mr. Gravelines says there are five villages nearby. Two are Mandan. Three are Hidatsa. In all, some four thousand people live in this area, far more than live in St. Louis or Washington. Mr. Gravelines says that in the late summer, Indians from the west travel here to trade

122

horses and furs with the Arikara, Tetons, Yanktons, and other Missouri River tribes. Any tribes at war declare a temporary peace for the trading season. Traders from St. Louis, New York, Canada, and even France, England, and Spain come here to buy furs.

The Captains hope we can spend a peaceful winter among these people. Yet we are greatly outnumbered. If the Mandan or Hidatsa attacked us, we would not stand a chance.

The Mandan rarely travel far from their villages, but Hidatsa hunting and raiding parties ride west all the way to the Rocky Mountains. Capt. Lewis is eager to meet the Hidatsa. He says they can tell us whether that old trader's map is right, whether we will need to buy Shoshone horses to cross that small stretch of the mountains.

Mr. Gravelines left us to go back to his family. Not long after, a French trader, Rene Jessaume, came to see us. He has lived with the Mandan for fifteen years and has a Mandan wife and children. Capt. Lewis hired him as an interpreter.

Mandan campsite
Oct. 29, '04

Whitehouse and I struggled against a howling gale to stretch the boat sail to make a windbreak. Then we all put on our uniforms. Soon Big White arrived with Black Cat, chief of the upper Mandan village. Several lesser chiefs came, too. Capt. Lewis had to shout, "Children!"

to be heard over the flapping sail. After the speech, Big White and Black Cat smoked the peace pipe with Man Wolf. There is peace at last between the Mandan and the Arikara.

Later Big White told Capt. Lewis that his people are glad to have peace with the Arikara. Now the men can hunt without fear. Now the women can work the fields without looking over their shoulders, always on guard for the enemy.

Four of the Hidatsa chiefs—Horned Weasel, Le Borgne (or One Eye, as he is called), Black Moccasin, and Little Fox—were invited to the council but did not come. So Capt. Lewis packed up gifts for them and asked Jessaume and Drewyer to deliver them. The Captain sent especially fine presents to One Eye, who heads the biggest and northernmost Hidatsa village. He is known as a powerful leader. Capt. Lewis badly wants to meet this One Eye.

Lightning set off a prairie fire this evening. The wind swept the flames so close to our camp that we could feel the heat. We were lucky it passed us by.

Mandan campsite
Oct. 31, '04

Collins and I went hunting and stumbled on some-thing of a miracle. Walking through the burned prairie grass, we came upon two charred bodies, burned to death in last night's fire. Near them we saw a badly seared buffalo skin. Collins thought he saw some movement under the hide. He lifted it and there, curled in a ball, was a young boy no more than two years old. I picked him up and he began to cry, but only from fright, for when I looked him over, I was amazed to find he was not at all burned. The bodies must have been his parents. Their last act when caught in the fire was to cover their son with the hide of a freshly killed buffalo, hoping to save him. We carried the boy to Big White's village, where he was taken in.

Chief Black Cat and some of his men sat at our campfire tonight. Black Cat wore the dress uniform we gave him, including the three-cornered hat. He looks fine in this gear. Saint Peter played his fiddle, and we danced a reel for our guests. All was friendly. Then York appeared. Black Cat jumped up. He shouted to his men and they quickly strung their bows and took aim at York. Capt. Lewis gestured wildly for them not to shoot, and at last all calmed down. Then Jessaume told us that Mandan braves paint their whole bodies black before going to war. Black Cat and his men believed that York had come to kill them. Poor York was shaken by this incident.

***

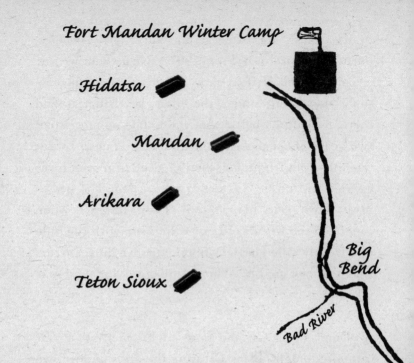

Fort Mandan Winter Camp

Hidatsa

Mandan

Arikara

Teton Sioux

Big Bend

Bad River

Mandan campsite
Nov. 2, '04

Capt. Lewis asked me to walk with him. We went to a high hill across the river from Big White's village. The Captain told me this is where we will build our winter fort. He has worked out the design. Two rows of cabins will be set at right angles to each other. An 18 foot fence will connect them, making the base of a triangle. A guard post will be set into the fence, with our swivel gun mounted on top. Inside the fence will be a plaza for our councils with the Indians. Capt.

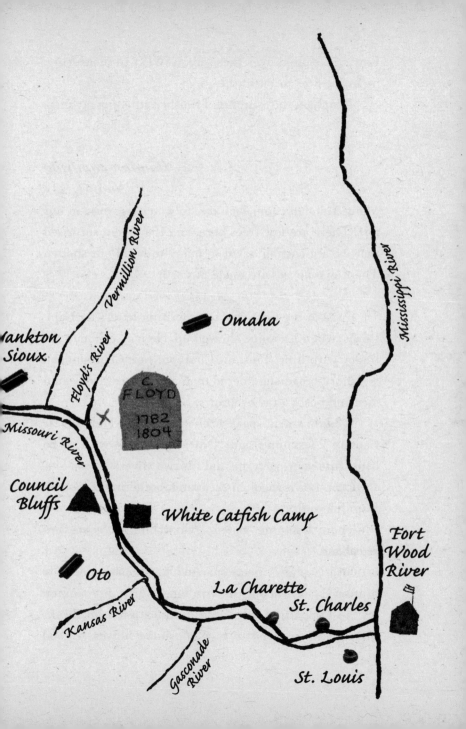

Lewis is excited over these plans. Next to measuring, he most loves to build things.

Tonight at the campfire, I finished stitching my map.

Mandan campsite
Nov. 4, '04

Many Mandan come each day to watch us work on our fort. There are few trees here, and they seem surprised that we are cutting down so many to build our shelter. Their own houses are made of earth.

I was in the Captains' tent, writing letters for Capt. Lewis, when Jessaume showed up. He had a French fur trader with him, Toussant Charbonneau. Charbonneau is a short, broad-shouldered man with a weather-beaten face and bushy gray eyebrows.

"Charbonneau speak French and little Hidatsa, Sir Captain," Jessaume said. "No English. He wish to be hired into your party, he and his two wives."

Capt. Lewis shook his head, not bothering to look up from his work.

Then Jessaume added, "Charbonneau wives are Shoshone."

The Captain's head snapped up. "Shoshone?" He muttered some about the wisdom of bringing women on the Expedition, but I could almost see him thinking that if we need to buy Shoshone horses, a good interpreter could help him bargain.

"Hired," Capt. Lewis told Charbonneau. "At $25 a month. You may bring along one wife. Only one."

Mandan campsite
Nov. 5, '04

I spent this day some 100 yards off from the huts, digging a privy.

This evening, when I went to the Captains' tent to copy over letters for him, I found him pacing.

"Why has not one single Hidatsa come to see us, Pup?" he said. "Why? Why?"

He is desperate to talk with someone who has traveled west, but the Hidatsa, it seems, want nothing to do with the Corps of Discovery.

Mandan campsite
Nov. 6, '04

In the middle of the night, Sgt. Pryor blew his horn for an alarm. We all leaped up, grabbed our rifles, and ran out of our tents, expecting to find arrows flying. But Sgt. Pryor had gotten us up to see an amazing spectacle in the skies. I thought Capt. Lewis might reprimand him for his action, but the Captain was giddy with delight at seeing what he says are the Northern Lights. We all got our blankets and spread them out. Then we laid back with our hands beneath our heads and watched as strange glowing colors—green, blue, orange—lit up the heavens. The lights dimmed, almost disappearing, then burst forth again, more brilliant than ever. Only when we were sure the show was over did we go back to our tents, so happy to have seen such a wonder.

One of Charbonneau's Shoshone wives came to our camp. She is small, dark skinned, and serious. She wore a fine buffalo robe, with the fur side in for warmth, and carried two more robes. Drewyer signed with her and discovered that these robes are gifts for the Captains.

After she left, Drewyer told us her name is Sacagawea, which in English means something close to "boat pusher." Charbonneau has picked her as the one wife to come with him on our journey. Drewyer says Sacagawea is young, maybe 15 or 16. She and Charbonneau's other wife, Otter Woman, were captured four years ago by Horned Weasel, then a brave, who led a raiding party against the Shoshone, killing many of them. Horned Weasel took the girls back to his village, where they worked as slaves until Charbonneau won them from him in a gambling game. Drewyer says it looks to him as if Sacagawea will soon bear a child.

I wonder if Capt. Lewis knows about *that*.

Freezing weather. Capt. Lewis led a party of us over the frozen river to hunt. We killed eleven buffalo, but they were all bones, no meat.

I was copying letters when Sgt. Ordway brought Sacagawea to Capt. Lewis's tent. She carried four more buffalo robes and gave them to the Captain. I tried to sign, asking if she had stitched these robes herself, but she only looked away. I wonder who will get the robes.

The Captain gave the buffalo robes to the three sergeants and to Drewyer. How good it must feel to wear a thick, woolly robe in this bitter cold.

Chief Big White and his wife came to visit. She carried 100 pounds of meat as a gift for us.

***

Mandan campsite
Nov. 14, '04

Snowing. The 100 pounds of meat are eaten. Now we have only salt pork.

Fort Mandan
Nov. 16, '04

Woke to find the trees coated with ice. We struck our tents and moved into our huts before we, too, became ice coated. The huts are only half finished, but they will keep us warmer than the tents. I share a hut with the others from my mess. Charbonneau and his wives moved into a hut of their own.

Fort Mandan
Nov. 19, '04

Today Collins, McNeal, and I worked to seal the walls of the smokehouse by daubing clay into the cracks between the logs. Just in time, too. The hunting party returned with 32 deer, 11 elk, and 1 buffalo. Colter shot a very large bobcat.

Fort Mandan
Nov. 20, '04

Each morning I go to the Captains' hut to copy over

journal pages that one or both of them wrote the day before. Capt. Lewis wants a copy, should the originals be lost or destroyed.

This morning as I copied, Jessaume came to see the Captain.

"The Mandan tell untrue stories to the Hidatsa, Sir Captain," Jessaume said. "Stories to make them believe you are their enemy."

Capt. Lewis's jaw dropped open. "But why?" he asked.

"The Mandan want to keep Hidatsa away, Sir Captain," said Jessaume. "Then they will have all your trade goods for themselves."

Capt. Lewis jumped up, threw on his buffalo robe, and set off for the Hidatsa villages to put things right. He took Jessaume and Charbonneau with him to translate.

Capt. Lewis has returned. I have never seen him so low. When he arrived at Horned Weasel's village, the chief sent word that he was "not at home." It was the same in all three villages. None of the chiefs would see him.

I pried the Captain's feet out of his icy boots. He said his toes felt frosted and asked me to fill a pail with cool water so he might soak them. I feel so bad for him, walking miles in the snow and freezing his toes, all for nothing.

Colter is the envy of every man in our party. He skinned the head of the bobcat he shot, lined it with fur, and made it fit him snugly for a hat. He fashioned it to look as if the bobcat's mouth is wide open, and his face is poking out from it. The bobcat ears stick up on top of his head. No man ever had a finer hat. Colter also made himself a pair of bobcat gloves, lined with fur.

Bobcats, beware! Every man in our party is gunning for you now. Yet in this miserable freezing cold weather, I would rather have a buffalo robe to warm not only my head, but all of me.

Woke with achy joints. My neck was too stiff to turn my head. Capt. Lewis heated a stone in the fire, wrapped it in flannel, and set it on my neck. This helped considerable, and by midday I was braiding strips of elk skin together to make a rope for hauling the keelboat out of the river.

Capt. Lewis thinks only of meeting with One Eye. He believes this chief can open the door to all other Hidatsa chiefs. The Captain is always plotting what gifts he might give to win over this mighty ruler.

Capt. Lewis set off for the Hidatsa villages again this morning. He took Jessaume, Charbonneau, and loads of gifts with him.

Unlucky Capt. Lewis! Not long after he left, three Hidatsa chiefs appeared at our fort. York made a meal for them, but Capt. Lewis had taken our only two Hidatsa interpreters with him, so Capt. Clark and the chiefs had no way to talk with one another. After they ate, the chiefs went home again.

I was standing guard when I spied a party coming toward the fort. Capt. Lewis was in the lead, and even at a great distance I could tell he was in fine spirits. Soon after, Capt. Lewis led two Hidatsa chiefs, Black Moccasin and Little Fox, into our fort. These chiefs had believed the false stories spread by the Mandan. They were told we had joined forces with the Sioux and planned to cut off their winter supplies. Now Capt. Lewis has set them straight.

Around the fire this evening, with Charbonneau interpreting, Capt. Lewis asked these chiefs to make peace with the Shoshone, the Blackfeet, and all other nations. Black Moccasin and Little Fox gave their word to do so. We celebrated this promise of peace with fiddling and dancing. Collins showed off by dancing on his hands. Capt. Lewis cannot stop smiling.

Fort Mandan
Nov. 29, '04

Once more Jessaume is the bearer of bad news. He came to Capt. Lewis's hut to report that a society of young Hidatsa warriors, who call themselves the Wolves, have ridden out in a raid against the Blackfeet. Capt. Lewis sprang up, all in a fury. He said he must talk to Black Moccasin and Little Fox at once. He asked me to go along, and we set out with Jessaume for the Hidatsa villages. Capt. Lewis walked so fast, I could hardly keep up with him. As he went, he muttered darkly about "false promises."

When we arrived, we were taken to see the chiefs. Capt. Lewis demanded to know why they had not kept their promise of peace.

When Black Moccasin understood the Captain's words, he looked surprised. Through Jessaume, he explained that a raid is not a war. A raid is the way a young warrior earns his glory. Without raids and glory, Little Fox added, how would we know which man to pick for a chief?

I thought of what Drewyer told me about Horned

Weasel. He had led a raiding party to the west and killed many Shoshone. He had captured Sacagawea and Otter Woman. Now he was chief.

Capt. Lewis tried to argue, but the Hidatsa chiefs seemed confused by his words.

At last we tramped back to our fort.

"Glory, my foot," Capt. Lewis grumbled. "Have you ever earned any glory, Pup?"

"No, sir," I said. "The only thing I have ever earned is a place on this Expedition, and I did that not by any raid, but by toting a dead heavy keelboat over every sandbar in the Ohio River." I shook my head. "There is not much glory in that."

"None, Pup," agreed Capt. Lewis, and he laughed.

I was glad to have raised his spirits some.

Fort Mandan
Nov. 30, '04

Worse news this morning! A Mandan brave ran to our fort. He said that the Arikara and Sioux had banded together and attacked a Mandan hunting party. One Mandan hunter was killed and two others were wounded. The raiders stole nine horses.

Capt. Clark quickly lined twenty-three of us up. We shouldered our guns and marched military style out of our fort. It was hard going through knee-deep snow on the ice-covered river, and even harder slogging through the snow-covered brush, but at last we reached Big White's village. The chief seemed startled at the sight of us, all armed and at his door.

Capt. Clark told him we were ready to chase down the Arikara and Sioux who had attacked his people. He asked if the chief wanted to send any braves out with us.

Through Jessaume, Chief Big White replied: "It is too cold to go after the raiders, and the snow is too deep. Vengeance can wait until spring." The chief folded his arms across his chest. "You promised peace between the Arikara and the Mandan," he went on. "Because of this promise, I believed it was safe to let my people go out to hunt. Now look what has happened! One man is dead. Two more may soon join him."

I could see it his way. No wonder the chief was angry.

Capt. Clark went into Big White's lodge. He stayed there, talking with the chief, for over two hours. We men waited outside, hungry, cold, and miserable. It was dark by the time we began our march back through the freezing snow.

When we reached our fort, Capt. Clark poured each of us a drink of hot rum. I sipped mine and wondered: Did President Jefferson have any idea how hard it would be to make peace among the Indians?

* * *

Chief Big White is no longer angry. This morning he sent word that gangs of buffalo have been seen on nearby hills. He invited us to join his people in a hunt. We badly need meat, so in spite of the bitter weather, Capt. Lewis picked twelve men to hunt, and I was one of them. It was hard to leave my warm hut for the frigid air, yet I felt proud. Seven months ago, I had not shot a single deer. Now I bring in meat for the party fairly regular.

We marched out on foot. The Mandan rode ponies bareback, steering with their knees while galloping at astonishing speeds. This left both hands free to shoot their bows. Each time a buffalo fell, Mandan women quickly ran to it so as to beat the wolves, and butchered it on the spot.

Our party killed ten buffalo, but the wolves got five. We packed what meat we could carry on our backs and marched home to the fort.

Colder yet! Seaman left the hut only to relieve himself, then ran quickly back inside.

Capt. Clark led men out hunting and did not return until after dark. Several men froze their feet. York took a pee in the frigid wind, and now complains that his private parts are frosted. Yet the party shot plenty of game, too much to carry back to the fort. Collins and Joseph Fields are now camped with the meat to guard it from the wolves. Poor men, out all night in this icy weather.

Fort Mandan
24 degrees below zero
Dec. 10, '04

The frostbit are recovering. I am helping Sgt. Gass build sleds for hauling meat.

Capt. Clark shot a bobcat. Colter says what a shame its head is too small to make a hat.

Fort Mandan
42 degrees below zero
Dec. 12, '04

So, so cold! Our only work was fetching wood to keep our fires burning.

Capt. Clark stuck his head into our hut and said, "Until the weather warms, we will change the guard every hour."

When it came my turn, I thought Seaman would stick by me, as usual, but he only walked with me to the door of the hut. He was wise, for even breathing is painful in this weather. Freezing air burned my throat. My chest felt as if it were icing up inside. I had to keep marching and waving my arms the whole time I stood guard so as not to freeze. That one hour felt far longer than the usual three.

Fort Mandan
24 degrees
Dec. 19, '04

Warm weather! Worked outside all day, helping to set up our picket fence.

I went to the Captains' hut this afternoon and found Capt. Lewis with Jessaume and two Mandan. They were hunched over the old trader's map. Through Jessaume, one Mandan said he had heard that crossing the Rocky Mountains on horseback takes half a day. Capt. Lewis nodded. Just what the old trader had said. It looks as if the Captain will have to buy horses from the Shoshone. It looks as if the Northwest Passage has a short stretch of land between the rivers.

Fort Mandan
Dec. 22, '04

Still working on the pickets.

Several Mandan squaws came to trade with us today.

With them were a number of men dressed as squaws. Jessaume says these men are highly prized by the Mandan, as they are said to receive dreams of prophecy from a mysterious spirit power.

Fort Mandan
Dec. 24, '04

Deep snow all around us this Christmas Eve. I think of Pa. I miss him terrible.

Finished our picket fence. Now I am helping to set up a blacksmith shop.

This evening, the Captains came by each hut and gave out dried meat, flour, pepper, and apples. We will add them to our stew pots to make our Christmas supper.

Fort Mandan
Christmas Day, '04

At daybreak, we hoisted the American flag and fired our cannon. Then each of us shot off our guns in turn. Midday, our Captains gave a party. They poured us each a drink of hot rum, and we ate our stew. John Collins carried in what he called Drunken Cherry Dessert, made from the cherries he put into the whiskey barrel all those months ago. The taste of those cherries took us back to summer days on the prairie when we had gathered them, and warmed our spirits.

142

Fort Mandan
Dec. 31, '04

No sooner was the blacksmith shop finished than the Mandan lined up at our fort bringing axes, kettles, and other metal items in need of repair. It is my job to collect the tools, etc., and take them to Shields, who heats them, then pounds the hot metal with his hammer, making sparks fly. For this service, the Mandan pay us with beans, squash, bread, and dried corn. The game we shoot is lean and quickly eaten. We are thankful for the Mandan food.

This afternoon, Collins, Colter, and I walked as far as Black Cat's village looking for trees to make into dugout canoes, but found none big enough. Seaman trotted along at my side as we went. On the way back to the fort, I saw blood on the snow and discovered that the dog's footpads were cracked and bleeding from walking on the icy ground.

I am stitching leather booties to protect Seaman's paws.

Fort Mandan
Jan. 1, 1805

We celebrated the new year by tooting our tin horns as we marched across the frozen river to Big White's village. The Mandan led us to their main lodge. Saint Peter started fiddling and the Mandan played drums, tambourines, and deer-hoof rattles. We all danced together for hours. Just when we thought we could dance no more, Saint Peter began to play his fiddle faster and faster. We began to dance faster. Then, one by one, dancers dropped away, as they could not keep up with the music. I stayed in until my legs got tangled up and I tripped on my own feet. Only York could do steps quick enough. He kept it up as long as Saint Peter played. When the tune ended, we all cheered him.

Fort Mandan
Jan. 4, '05

I put the leather booties I made on Seaman's paws so he could walk with me in the snow. But the dog's tail drooped, he lowered his head, and he collapsed on the ground. Colter hooted with laughter when he saw him hunkered down so miserable. I tried to coax him, but the dog would not get up until I took off his boots.

I visited the Fields brothers in their hut. They proudly showed me their pets. They have three squawking magpies. Also a small chickenlike creature called a grouse. And the little dog Capt. Lewis captured by pouring water into its burrow. The little dog was curled up, sleeping. Joseph said this is what he would be doing now in his den under the snow. Come spring, Capt. Lewis will send these examples of western animals to Washington. If President Jefferson is expecting sabertooth tigers and 7 foot beavers, he may be disappointed.

Chief Big White invited us to a Mandan buffalo dance. This dance is done to call the buffalo close so the Mandan can kill them.

Buffalo have been spotted near the river. Were they called by the dance? I badly want to go out with the hunting party and get one so I can make myself a warm buffalo robe.

A thirteen-year-old Mandan boy stayed out all night without a fire and his feet froze. His father carried him to our fort. I ran to fetch a bowl of cool water to soak his feet, then called Capt. Lewis. When the Captain saw the boy's toes, he shook his head. He says they are badly frosted.

Whitehouse and I came out hunting for buffalo. Before long, we hope to be wrapped up in our own woolly buffalo robes. We left the fort midday, heading south. Whitehouse shot three elk and I got four. At last we saw buffalo tracks in the snow. We followed them until the sun went down and then made camp. We butchered two of the elk, hanging the meat on trees to protect it from the wolves, which we hear all around us, howling.

Only those parts of us right up next to the fire keep warm. All the rest is so very cold. The wind is terrible. Can a storm be coming?

Near Fort Mandan
Jan. 11, '05

A blizzard hit last night. Whitehouse's feet froze in his sleep. When he woke, he could not walk or even move his toes. He is not in pain, only numb. I melted snow over the fire to make cool water to soak his feet, but when I took the water off the fire, it froze instantly in the pan.

Whitehouse is too heavy for me to carry to the fort. He says I must go back and bring help. How can I leave him here alone?

I have done as Whitehouse asked. I am on my way to get help. Before I left, I stacked firewood and cut up plenty of elk meat for him. I packed a small portion for myself and set off for the fort. I had only walked for a short spell when another blizzard struck. All I could do was hunker down on the leeward side of a hill and wait out the fierce winds. Hard not to think of Pa and the blizzard that froze him so cruelly between the barn and our house.

At last the wind and snow let up some. Dark was coming on, so I made camp. I am so worried for Whitehouse. Can he have kept his fire going in the storm?

Near Fort Mandan
Jan. 12, '05

The storm is over, all is still. The sun shines so bright on the white snowy ground that looking at it hurts my eyes.

Ate the last of my food. Must get my bearings before I go on. But the river and the valley have vanished under mounds of snow. Which way is the fort from here? I cannot tell.

Where am I?
Jan. 13, '05

Trudged through waist-deep snow all day, using the sun as my compass. No sign of the fort. No man, no animal. Only snow. Can Whitehouse be hanging on? He is counting on me to bring help. It is growing dark again and I am lost and so ashamed.

Nowhere
Jan. 15, '05

Morning. Sky filling with clouds. Another blizzard? I keep walking. If I stop, I will die.

Stumbled into Mandan hunting camp. Two women there, scraping buffalo skins. I put my hand to my mouth, signing, *I need food!* The older woman went to a kettle hanging over a fire, poured soup into a bowl, and carried

147

it to me. The scent of the soup fired up my hunger. I had just cupped my trembling hands around the warm bowl and was bringing it to my mouth when the woman who had brought it to me leaned forward and spat into the soup. I jerked back. What sort of monster was she? I felt sick, no longer hungry, but I had to eat. I slid my fingers into the soup at the edge of the bowl, away from her spittle, and brought them to my mouth. I ate slowly, licking soup from my fingers. At last my stomach settled. I stopped shaking. The whole time I ate, the fiendish woman stood nearby, nodding and smiling. She seemed to enjoy the sight of me struggling to get my fill.

Sitting by the fire a moment, I gathered warmth and strength for my journey. The soup brought me back to my senses. I know this hunting camp. Our fort is directly west of here.

I have reached our fort! I went straight to Capt. Lewis and told him of Whitehouse's frosted feet. I said I must go back to him. The Captain said he would send other, fitter men. But I said I must go as well, as I cannot rest until Whitehouse is here with me. At last he gave me leave. Colter, Collins, and I will set off at dawn with a sled.

Whitehouse has been alone for three days and three nights in the brutal cold, surrounded by wolves. I am so afraid we will not get to him in time.

***

Whitehouse is alive! We found him curled beside the coals of his fire. The fuel I cut for him had just run out. He had managed to pull himself around enough to reach the meat and cook it. In the three days I was gone, he ate most of an elk.

Collins and Colter wrapped Whitehouse in a buffalo robe. They picked him up and put him on the meat sled. We pulled him back to the fort, arriving after dark. Capt. Lewis treated his feet. He thinks his toes can be saved.

Whitehouse sits beside me now at the campfire. He is wrapped in his own buffalo robe. He is in good spirits, so thankful to have survived. He even joked that the freezing was worth it to get a robe. What with keeping his fire lit and holding the wolves at bay, he said the time passed swiftly. Last night he saw an eclipse of the moon.

Seaman sits on my other side. The dog has not left me since I returned.

A few men ribbed me some for being lost again, but no man claimed he could have done better in a blizzard. I told the story of coming across the hunting camp, half starved. How the Mandan woman spit in my soup, how she must be some sort of demon.

Drewyer spoke up. "What happens when a starving man bolts his food?"

"He pukes up what he ate and grows weaker," answered Joseph Fields.

We all nodded, agreeing that this was so.

"You do not understand Mandan, Shannon," Drewyer said. "The squaw had no way to tell you not to eat too fast, so she found another way to curb your hunger."

I believe Drewyer is right. This would account for the woman smiling as I licked the soup from my fingers. If he is right, then this woman saved me, and saved Whitehouse as well.

After this exchange Saint Peter started fiddling. I jumped up and danced around the campfire with the others. I hope Whitehouse will soon be dancing, too.

Fort Mandan
Jan. 20, '05

I am always hungry. All the men are hungry. We have so little meat. We are living on Mandan corn.

Fort Mandan
Jan. 26, '05

The blood has come back into Whitehouse's toes. He can walk now with only a small limp.

The Mandan boy brought here with frostbit feet is not so lucky. Capt. Lewis examined him today. One foot is healing, but all five toes on the other are rotting. They must come off, or he will lose the foot. The

Captain asked me to help him with the removal. I got a sick feeling in my gut but said I would. I gave the boy a good amount of whiskey. When he grew sleepy, I gripped his hand and gave a nod to Capt. Lewis. He picked up his saw. The boy squeezed my hand tight. He kept his eyes fastened on mine as the Captain began sawing off his toes. He never made a sound. I thought I might pass out, but the boy was so brave, I had to be brave, too.

Fort Mandan
Jan. 27, '05

No Mandan have come to our blacksmith shop this week. All their pots, kettles, and knives are repaired. We are out of business. And out of Mandan corn. We are all so very hungry.

Fort Mandan
Jan. 29, '05

Capt. Lewis is pacing. Shields has told him that the Mandan want double-bladed battle-axes. He says he can make these axes and trade them for corn.

"We are desperate for food," the Captain said to me. "But our mission is to make peace among the Indians, not weapons for them to use against each other. President Jefferson would not approve."

151

One Eye and Horned
Weasel's village

Little Fox and
Black Moccasin's
village

White Buffalo
Robe's village

My hunger made me bold. I said, "President Jefferson is not here in the frozen wilderness faced with feeding some thirty men each day."

I am helping Shields cut up the metal stove. He will turn the metal into axes. The Mandan have agreed to pay 8 gallons of corn per axe. As long as axes are in demand, we will not starve.

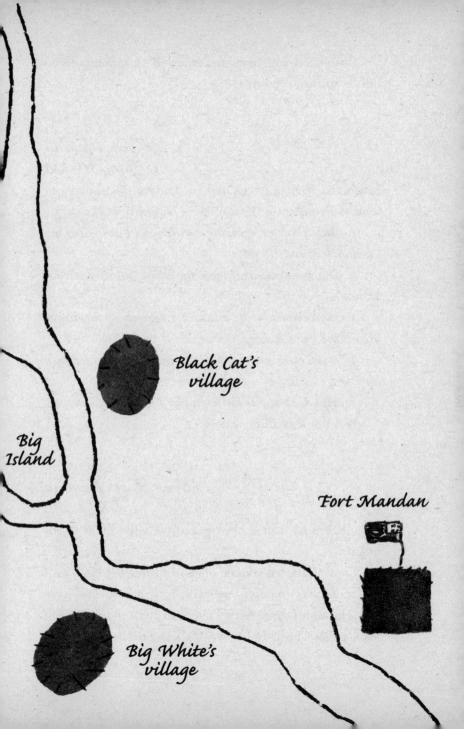

Black Cat's
village

Big
Island

Fort Mandan

Big White's
village

I finished my map and showed it around. Even Colter admired the stitching.

Little Fox is helping us make a Hidatsa vocabulary to send to President Jefferson. Here is how it works:

1. Little Fox says a Hidatsa word, and I write it down the way it sounds.

2. Charbonneau translates the word into French for Jessaume.

3. Charbonneau and Jessaume bicker about the meaning of the French word.

4. Finally Jessaume translates the word into English for Capt. Lewis.

5. Capt. Lewis tells me what word to write down.

It is not a surefire system.

Corn keeps us from starving, but we need meat to fill us up.

Capt. Clark led sixteen of us out hunting. He says if we travel far enough, we will find game. We have brought along three horses and two sleds to carry meat back to the fort. Today we walked on the ice for 22 miles, but saw no game. We are camped now and have nothing to eat.

Hunting trip
Feb. 5, '05

Very cold and windy. We are 44 miles from the fort. Capt. Clark stepped through the ice and wet his legs up to the knee. Now he cannot stop shivering. I shot a buffalo, but there was hardly any meat on him, and his coat was too poor to make a robe.

Hunting
Feb. 7, '05

Hunting has picked up. Our bellies are full. We are butchering buffalo and packing up the meat.

We packed our meat onto the sleds and onto the backs of our horses. Charbonneau and I left our hunting camp at dawn, walking through knee-deep snow, leading the horses back to the fort. It was a long trip and hard going. At last we reached the bottom of the hill below our fort. The horses cannot climb up the icy hill, so Charbonneau has gone up to the fort to get men to carry up the meat. I am waiting with the horses.

Three hours waiting for Charbonneau. Where can he be? I jump and stomp and dance to keep my blood moving. I keep the horses moving, too, so they will not get frosted. Can Charbonneau have forgot about us?

Six men arrived with sleds. Charbonneau never told them I was waiting. They spied me from the fort on their own. Yet Charbonneau can be forgiven, for when he reached the fort, he found Sacagawea laboring to give birth to their child.

I am working inside the Captains' hut. I can hear Sacagawea screaming in pain. Otter Woman is with her. Charbonneau sits outside the hut, crying and begging the Captains to do something. He is pulling out his hair, he is so desperate. When Ma labored so hard with little Wilson, Pa had a terrible haunted look in his eyes, just as Charbonneau does now, but there was nothing he could do.

At last Capt. Lewis went to see if he could help. He came back looking grim.

"She cannot push the child forth," he said.

"Is there nothing in your medicine kit to help her?" I asked.

The Captain shook his head. "Dr. Rush never imagined we would need medicine for childbirth," he said. "If she keeps going like this much longer, she will die."

Sacagawea!

Fort Mandan
Feb. 11, '05

It is quiet now. Sacagawea is too weak to scream. Yet her child has not come. Capt. Lewis is pacing and muttering. He feels as helpless as Charbonneau.

Jessaume appeared at the door of the hut.

"Sir Captain," he said, "Mandan women who cannot bring forth find helpful to drink rattlesnake tail, ground to powder, mixed with warm water."

Capt. Lewis frowned and said, "If only we had some."

"We do!" I said, and I ran for the medicine kit,

remembering how Capt. Clark had put rattles in it. I brought them to Capt. Lewis. He crumbled three rings into a cup and added water from the kettle on his fire. Then he rushed off to take this potion in to Sacagawea.

A son has been born to Sacagawea and Charbonneau! Not ten minutes after Capt. Lewis went into her hut with the rattler tea, we heard a baby's cry. All of us men burst out cheering.

Capt. Lewis carried the baby out of the hut, wrapped in an American flag, for all to see. He held him up, declaring, "This boy is born an American!"

"Jean Baptiste!" cried Charbonneau, standing beside the Captain. "Jean Baptiste Charbonneau!"

Jean Baptiste is healthy, and so is his mother. We are all so glad!

Fort Mandan
Feb. 13, '05

Jean Baptiste cried in the night. I was half asleep, dreaming I was home, with little Wilson fretting. I woke, surprised to find myself in a hut with six snoring men. How I ache to see my baby brother. I miss the big boys, too. And Nancy and Lavinia. Oh, Thomas, I hope Ma never sent you to Uncle Liam.

All those pounds of meat Charbonneau and I carried

back through the snow are eaten. Now we are hungry again.

Capt. Clark came back from hunting, saying his party had great success. Drewyer and a crew are guarding the game, building pens to keep it safe from wolves. Bratton and three others have set out from the fort with horses and sleds to bring us the meat.

Fort Mandan
Feb. 14, '05

Drewyer ran back to the fort calling out that his party had been attacked by Teton Sioux! The Tetons raided the meat pen. They cut the bridles on two of our horses, jumped on their backs, and rode off. Bratton managed to keep hold of Lizzy.

We are going after these raiders. Capt. Clark sent word to Big White. He asked for men to help us. The chief and several braves came right away. We leave at sunup.

Fort Mandan
Feb. 16, '05

Marched 30 miles over snow and ice yesterday, searching for those Tetons. All we found was an abandoned sled and an empty meat pen. My blood is boiling. All of

159

us men are charged up to keep going after those thieving Tetons and get back our meat, but Capt. Lewis says
it is no use.

All right, Tetons. We will let you have that meat.
But we are the Corps of Discovery, and tomorrow we
will discover every living deer and elk and buffalo on
this land, and we will shoot them down!

Fort Mandan
Feb. 21, '05

Returned to the fort today, lugging some 2,400 pounds
of meat. We will not go hungry!

Fort Mandan
Feb. 24, '05

Charbonneau strutted around the fort today, showing
off Jean Baptiste. Capt. Clark patted the boy's head
and said, "Fine little pomp."

The icy river is starting to thaw.

Fort Mandan
Feb. 28, '05

I stitched up a tiny pair of moccasins for Pomp. (Capt.
Clark's nickname has stuck.) Colter saw me working on
them and said he hopes they are better received than

Seaman's booties. Later he brought me blue beads so I could add decoration. Today I gave the beaded moccasins to Charbonneau. He seemed pleased and insisted that I come and see the boy. Jean Baptiste lay sleeping beside his mother on a blue blanket. Sacagawea looked so proud. I tried to sign, "You have a fine son," but I must have got the signs wrong, for Sacagawea put a hand to her mouth and laughed.

Fort Mandan
March 9, '05

Whitehouse found my journal! He said it was in the smokehouse. It must have tumbled out of my possible bag. I am glad to have it, for I must stay off my feet a few days longer and writing will give me something to do beside stitching new moccasins for the entire Corps.

Three days back, I was hollowing out a tree for a canoe with a newly sharpened adze. My hand slipped, and I pitched forward, driving the adze into my foot. Blood spurted out from a deep gash. Colter and Collins carried me to Capt. Lewis. He tied a kerchief around my ankle to stop the bleeding, then put on salve and a bandage. He checked the wound today and says it is mending nicely.

I was copying pages with Capt. Lewis when Sgt. Ordway knocked on the door.

"We have visitors, Captain," Sgt. Ordway said. "Chief Le Borgne and his men."

Capt. Lewis jumped up so fast his journal pages went flying. He raced out of the hut, nearly crashing into Collins. He told Collins to get gifts for the chief. "Good ones!" he shouted after him.

By the time I hobbled out to the plaza, Capt. Lewis had already given gifts and was shooting his air gun. One Eye watched the demonstration with little expression on his lean, pockmarked face. His bad eye is not covered with a patch. I drew closer and saw that his eyelids had been stitched together.

Capt. Lewis held out his spyglass to the chief. One Eye waved it away. Capt. Lewis showed him our compass. One Eye shrugged. Then York walked past, on his way to the kitchen, and suddenly One Eye grew excited. He motioned York to come to him. The chief spoke rapidly to his men, exclaiming over York's color and curly hair. He turned poor York around. Then he spat on his fingers and rubbed York's skin, hard. He seemed surprised when no paint came off on his hand. York stood tall during this test of his color. He never pulled away nor showed any sign of anger, yet it must be hard to be a curiosity.

With Charbonneau interpreting, Capt. Lewis invited the chief to stay for a meal and tell him all about the land to the west. One Eye did not bother to reply. He signaled his men to pick up his gifts, and the

Hidatsa quickly left our fort.

Tonight, Capt. Lewis is pacing and muttering worse than ever.

Fort Mandan
March 11, '05

Charbonneau strutted into the Captains' hut today. Jessaume came along to translate.

"Charbonneau say he interpret fine with Chief Le Borgne," Jessaume told the Captains. "He say Captains counting on Sacagawea to get you good trade for Shoshone horses."

Capt. Lewis stared, as if not believing Jessaume's words.

"Charbonneau say you need him much, Sir Captains," said Jessaume. "From here on, Charbonneau no longer chop wood, cook, or stand guard. If food supplies run low, Charbonneau not hold back. He asks Sir Captains make these changes."

Capt. Clark reddened up as he listened.

Capt. Lewis stood. "A change will be made," he said, eyeing Charbonneau. "You will pack up and leave our fort at once."

Charbonneau's eyes grew wide with surprise.

"That is all," said Capt. Lewis, and he sat back down.

Not long after, the little family left our fort. Sacagawea carried Pomp on her back in his cradle board.

She carried most of their goods as well. Charbonneau dragged along behind like a big sad dog.

Sacagawea pitched their tent right outside our fort. I walked by it today and saw her preparing a meal. I stopped and tried my signs again, saying: "You have a fine son." This time, Sacagawea seemed to understand. She lifted the baby out of his cradle board and held him out to me. I took him in my arms. He looked at me with serious dark eyes. But when I said, "Pomp!" he broke into a toothless grin.

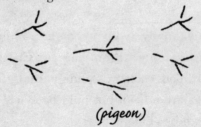

(pigeon)

The snow is melting. We are sunning our goods. The new canoes are nearly finished. We will soon be on our way! How different this winter has been from winter in Fort Wood River. There, the men quarreled and disobeyed the sergeants. Here, we have all worked together harmonious.

Charbonneau and Jessaume came to see Capt. Lewis.

"Charbonneau say he not know what made him talk so foolish, Sir Captain," Jessaume said. "He so sorry and ask to be hired back into party, no changes."

The Captain said, "I will think it over."

Fort Mandan
March 18, '05

Charbonneau, Sacagawea, and Pomp moved back into the fort today.

Fort Mandan
March 22, '05

The river is flowing again. Great slabs of ice race down its current.

We put the six new dugout canoes into the river. All are steady. No leaks.

Fort Mandan
March 30, '05

I limped down to the river today, the first time I have walked so far since my accident. Sgt. Gass set me to helping a crew mend the hull of the keelboat. As we worked, three buffalo came floating down the river standing on a cake of ice. They must have been crossing the river when the ice broke up, and now they are stuck. Right behind them came a pair of Mandan hunters, jumping skillfully from one ice block to another until they got close enough to shoot the unfortunate buffalo.

Little Fox came to see Capt. Lewis. He gave directions for the way west, and I took them down:

1. Go upriver until you reach a tall tree with an eagle's nest in its branches.

2. From this point, be on the lookout for Great Falls, a place of enormous beauty.

3. After Great Falls, travel on to Three Forks, where three rivers flow together into one.

4. After Three Forks, you will come to the spring where the Missouri River begins.

5. Just west of this are the Shining Mountains. (Known to us as the Rocky Mountains.)

The Captain is so pleased to have clear directions.

At campfire, Little Fox warned us that on our way west we will meet the White Bear, which is twice the size of any other bear, and most ferocious. Drewyer says trappers call it the Grizzly. Little Fox says before they hunt the White Bear, the Hidatsa paint their bodies black to summon spirit powers, just as they do when going to war against another Indian nation.

Capt. Lewis shrugged. With our rifles, he says, no bear is too big for us.

***

We put the keelboat back into the river, ready for its trip down to St. Louis. I helped the Fields brothers pack food for the magpies, the grouse, and the little dog who will be aboard. Reuben Fields asked Newman to take good care of the pets on the trip, and he said he would. Since his arrest, Newman has worked hard, kept clear of Reed, and never given any trouble. Last week he asked the Captains if he might go west with us after all, but the Captains said no.

I am writing to Ma one last time.

Collins drew a sketch of me. It is far better than the first, as it shows how I have filled out with muscles. Collins gave me his picture to send to Ma with my letter. In exchange, Collins spoke aloud a letter to his family, and I took it down.

Colter asked me to do for him as I had done for Collins. He said out a letter to his ma and pa, and I wrote it down. I am now the owner of one beaded antelope-skin headband.

Went hunting and came back with five elk. Colter says

I have become the Scourge of Elk in the West. I do not mind this title.

Fort Mandan
April 7, '05

I lined up on the riverbank with many Mandan, Hidatsa, and the others of the Corps to bid the keelboat farewell. I thought back to when Capt. Lewis proudly showed me this boat, only half built. Corporal Warfington believes the boat will be stopped by the Teton Sioux, but as it is not carrying any guns or whiskey, he says it will get through. I near had a lump in my throat as the men put their paddles in the water and set off down the river. We all hollered and cheered them on their way. Godspeed!

When the boat was out of sight, we thanked Chief Big White for letting us shelter near his village over the winter. He promised to take Capt. Lewis's advice and travel to Washington to meet President Jefferson. We said good-bye to Jessaume, Otter Woman, and our many Mandan friends and promised to stop here again on our way back east.

I am assigned to the white pirogue, so I hopped in. Others hopped into the red pirogue, or into one of the six dugouts. Then our little fleet set off up the river. Capt. Lewis and Seaman stood on shore, watching us go. They will walk to Black Cat's village, where we will pick them up.

The white pirogue will lead the way as we go. It is our sturdiest craft, so it is loaded with our most important cargo: medicines, gunpowder, navigation instruments, the Captains' portable writing desks, Capt. Clark's maps, Capt. Lewis's Scientific Notebooks, and all journals. It is also our safest craft, so in addition to York, Drewyer, and myself, the white pirogue is paddled by our nonswimmers, Potts, Gibson, and Charbonneau. Saint Peter is our pilot. The Captains, Sacagawea, Pomp, and Seaman will be our passengers.

Most of us are raring to go, but not all. Otter Woman and Sacagawea wept and clung to each other at their parting. At last Sacagawea, with Pomp on her back, stepped into the white pirogue, and we pulled away from the shore.

So far, we have had maps to show us the way. Now we will be making the maps as we venture into Parts Unknown.

Our westward party is made up of
Capts. Lewis and Clark;
Sgts. Ordway, Pryor, and Gass;
Pvts. Bratton, Collins, Colter, Cruzatte, J. Fields, R. Fields, Frazer, Gibson, Goodrich, Howard, Labiche, Lepage, McNeal, Potts, Shannon, Shields, Thompson, Warner, Whitehouse, Windsor, and Weiser;
Interpreters: Drewyer and Charbonneau;
Also, York, Sacagawea, and Pomp,
and our dog, Seaman.

We are off!

The mosquitoes welcomed us back to the river.

We are camped now. Most of us will sleep in bedrolls under the stars. The Captains, Drewyer, Charbonneau, Sacagawea, and Pomp will sleep inside a large buffalo-skin tepee. The Captains call it their Leather Lodge. It was put up in quick order tonight by Sacagawea.

Upper Mandan village
April 8, '05

We picked up Capt. Lewis and our dog from Black Cat's village this morning. The wind blew hard against us all day. I have not used my paddling muscles since fall. Tonight my arms and shoulders ache.

Missouri River
April 9, '05

Took a break from paddling and walked on shore. Sacagawea walked with me. She carried a long stick, which she poked into mouse holes as we went, often stooping down to dig out knobby roots. All this with a baby on her back! I signed to her. She only smiled and never answered back, yet I believe she understands far more than most of the men think.

We stopped to rest, and Sacagawea fed Pomp. When

she took him out of his cradle board, I was happy to see he was wearing the moccasins I stitched for him. After the feeding, I signed that I would like to hold Pomp, and Sacagawea let me. The baby grabbed my finger and held on tight. Not yet two months old, and so strong!

When our party made camp tonight, Sacagawea cooked the roots she had collected. She offered them to us for our supper. Drewyer says they are wild artichoke. They were most welcome, as our hunters came back empty-handed.

This evening Capt. Clark shot and wounded a beaver. Seaman bounded into the river to fetch it. He struggled with the animal for a while, then managed to shake the life out of it and swim it back to shore.

North of Knife River
April 13, '05

Close call today. Charbonneau had talked his way into steering the boat, which is not so much work as paddling. The wind was in our favor. We hoisted our sails and sped up the river at a fast clip. A fierce storm struck, very sudden. The boat rocked badly. We all know by now to turn the boat into the wind to steady her, but Charbonneau panicked. He shoved the tiller away from him, turning us broad-side to the wind. The sails filled, and the boat heeledway over to one side. Capt. Lewis dove for the tiller. Drewyer jumped up and quickly brought down the sails. Our craft righted itself. We were lucky.

Tonight at the campfire, Charbonneau stood up and gave a speech. Even without an interpreter, we all understood that he was boasting about how well he handled the boat in the storm, how no man could have done as well. The rest of the party shouted and pelted him with clods of earth until he sat back down.

Capt. Lewis is badly shaken by our near disaster. "We were 200 yards from shore when that squall hit, Pup," he said. "Had we overturned, Potts, Gibson, and Charbonneau would have drowned. And my journals would have washed overboard, gone forever."

Missouri River
April 14, '05

Spring has arrived. Elk, deer, antelope, and buffalo gather in great numbers to graze on the new grass. I walked on shore with Seaman and a skinny yellow dog appeared. She must have been left behind by some Indians. After some growling and bristling of hair, the two dogs began running and frolicking together. Seaman seems glad to have met this yellow dog.

***

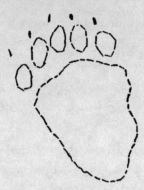

(white bear)

West of White Earth River
April 17, '05

Sgt. Ordway and I saw giant footprints on the riverbank. We think they were made by a White Bear. I will keep an eye on Seaman. He is no match for a grizzly.

The Fields brothers are feeding the yellow dog from their share of food. She is sticking with our party.

Missouri River
April 24, '05

The wind will not stop blowing. We all have sore eyes from the sand.

Tonight at supper, Seaman and the yellow dog were nowhere to be seen. Capt. Lewis and I called and called for Seaman. As yet he has not come running.

I cannot sleep for worrying over our dog. I hope he has not met a grizzly.

Missouri River
April 25, '05

Seaman and the yellow dog trotted into camp this morning, soaking wet and frisky. I hope wandering will not become Seaman's habit. I didn't get a minute's sleep last night.

Hunting is easy now. We shoot only what we need for each night's supper. Magnificent bald eagles circle overhead.

West of Yellowstone River
May 1, '05

Whitehouse and I went hunting. I shot a type of bird I had never seen before. I made the mistake of showing it to Capt. Lewis. I am now working to measure it, weigh it, and count every one of its feathers. The Captain says it may be a plover.

***

(porcupine)

Mouth of the Porcupine River
May 2, '05

We keep our eyes peeled for the sight of that eagle's nest. So far we have not seen it.

Passed a river with many porcupines scuttling along its banks. We named it accordingly.

Poor yellow dog. She stole some cooked meat and one of the men shot her. No one has owned up to the deed, but the Fields brothers are very angry. They say there is plenty of game for all. Seaman slunk off into the woods, miserable.

West of the Porcupine River
May 5, '05

Capt. Clark and Drewyer killed a tremendous grizzly and dragged it back to camp. They said it took many shots to bring the monster down. Capt. Lewis measured and said the bear stood nearly 9 feet tall. He estimates its weight at 600 pounds. We are awed by the sight of

175

this giant. When Drewyer cleaned it, he found the bear took twenty bullets.

Mouth of the Milk River
May 8, '05

We nooned it above the mouth of a large river. Its water was the color of tea with milk.

Joseph Fields is sick with a high fever. Capt. Lewis is treating him with Thunder Clappers.

Drewyer, Charbonneau, and Sacagawea went out seeking herbs. They brought back wild licorice and a root called white apple. Capt. Clark praised Sacagawea for helping our Expedition by bringing variety to our diet of meat, meat, and more meat. Drewyer signed to her what the Captain had said. Sacagawea nodded, knowing it is true.

West of Milk River
May 9, '05

Capt. Lewis shot a fat buffalo. Charbonneau said he would make a sausage from it which he calls by a French name, *boudin blanc*. I offered to help, and was rewarded by him handing me 6 feet of bulging buffalo intestine. Charbonneau showed me how to hold the gut tight with my right hand and press down with the fingers and thumb of my left hand, to squeeze out what it held. What it held smelled none too good, and Colter stood by, making jokes while I worked.

Next, I got the task of chopping up buffalo meat very fine. Charbonneau mixed this meat with salt, pepper, flour, and seasonings. Then he tied a knot in one end of the empty buffalo gut and showed me how to stuff the meat into it so that the outside of the gut ended up on the inside. I loaded that gut with the meat mixture until it was full to bursting. Charbonneau took it from me and knotted the other end. Then he ran with it down to the river, quickly dipped it into the water, ran back, and tossed it into a boiling kettle. (I never guessed Charbonneau could move so fast!) After it boiled, he cut the sausage into 1-foot lengths and threw them into a sizzling hot skillet. He fried the sausage in grizzly bear fat until it was nicely browned. The smell of it cooking caused every man (and dog) of our party to gather near. When it was done, Charbonneau sliced up the sausage and passed it around. He kept asking, "*Bon? Bon?*" And we all said, "Yes, *bon*! Very *bon*!" That *boudin blanc* was gone in no time, and we gave a hearty cheer for the chef. Charbonneau bowed and enjoyed his triumph.

Missouri River
May 11, '05

Hard spring rains have brought us a new danger. Without warning, cliffs collapse suddenly, sending huge masses of earth crashing down. We keep our boats to the middle of the river for safety. If a cliff were to fall on us, we would be buried alive.

Missouri River
May 13, '05

Wind too violent to paddle today. I went out with the hunting party. When we returned with several elk, Capt. Lewis's eyes lit up. "Elk hide is what I need to cover the frame of my iron boat," he said, and he set us to scraping the hides.

Missouri River
May 14, '05

Saint Peter spotted a grizzly on the shore this morning, and six of us went to get him. We snuck up close. At 40 paces, four of us raised our guns and fired. We all hit him, but this seemed only to annoy the bear. We hurried to reload while the other men shot. In the next round of shots, a ball hit the bear in the shoulder. Now he rose onto his hind feet, roaring in full fury. None of us had time to reload, so there was nothing for it but to turn tail and run. The bear galloped after us. Sgt. Ordway and Collins jumped in a canoe and paddled away. I ran into a willow thicket by a cliff with Whitehouse on my heels. I was reloading when the bear charged us. Whitehouse got off a shot. Yet still the grizzly came. The cliff was at our backs. The bear was barreling for us. Without thinking I threw down my gun and leaped over the cliff into the river. Whitehouse jumped in after me. We swam for the boats. I heard a loud splash behind, turned, and there came the bear, swimming after us! Our leather clothes soaked up water, making us heavy and slow. The bear was a rapid swimmer and quickly gained on us. Whitehouse was thrashing about, close to sinking. I turned to give the poor man a hand and saw that the bear was nearly on him. The grizzly's mouth was wide, roaring, filled with awful fangs. I thought I'd lost Whitehouse a second time when a shot rang out. The roaring stopped, very sudden. I looked up. There stood Colter atop the cliff, grinning. He had shot the beast in the head, killing him at last.

That bear was not so easy to bring in from the swift current, and even harder to lug ashore, but we did it. We found he had been hit by eight bullets. He was an old bear and tough, but we will eat his meat this night. We will render his fat for cooking grease. We have taken his fleece. Someone will get a warm coat out of our encounter with the grizzly.

All this before breakfast.

A day of adventure! Midday, I was rowing the white pirogue when a fierce wind struck. The boat began to pitch. How Charbonneau came to be sitting at the tiller again no one knows, but there he was. Just as before, he panicked, turning the boat sideways to the wind. She leaned to one side and water poured in. York and I leaned the opposite direction, trying to keep her from overturning. Charbonneau cried out. He let go of the tiller. Now the boat was swept about freely by the winds. Potts and Gibson kept their heads. They began bailing. York and I struggled to haul in the sail, but the wind was so violent, it whipped the ropes out of our hands.

Saint Peter was at the bow. He shouted in French to Charbonneau: *"Grab the tiller! Steer us into the wind!"*

Charbonneau only fell to his knees, crying out to his god to save him: *"Mon dieu! Mon dieu!"*

Potts tried to take the tiller, but the praying Charbonneau blocked his way. All was confusion. The pirogue was taking on water fast. The Captains' writing desks floated into the river. The tin boxes with the journals followed. The measuring instruments, everything not tied down, drifted out to be swept away in the current. There was much shouting. Only Sacagawea thought to catch what items she could as they floated by her. Each one she grabbed, she secured under the benches.

Another minute and we would have sunk, but Saint Peter grabbed his rifle. He aimed it at Charbonneau. He yelled in French, but his meaning was clear: *"Pick up the tiller or I'll blow your head off!"*

Charbonneau quickly picked up the tiller. At once

the boat righted itself, but it was nearly filled with water. We all began bailing, using pots and kettles, anything within reach, while York and Drewyer rowed us to the riverbank.

Both Captains had been walking on shore and could only watch, frantic, as the boat nearly went down. They helped us pull the boat up onto the rocks. We unloaded everything, and Capt. Lewis took stock. We lost some bedding, food, papers, and all the books got wet, but thanks to Sacagawea's calm head and quick action, the journals and writing desks and many other articles were saved. No one was drowned, for which we are mighty thankful.

The Captains served us hot rum tonight.

"From here on out, my journal will ride in the white pirogue," Capt. Lewis announced. "Capt. Clark's will go in the red. And Drewyer? Make it clear to Charbonneau that if he so much as touches the tiller again, I personally will shoot him."

Missouri River
May 15, '05

Still no sign of that eagle's nest.

At every bend in the river, Capt. Lewis peers ahead, hoping to spy the Shining Mountains in the distance. He had expected to see them by now.

Colter came to supper tonight wearing a handsome grizzly claw necklace.

Seaman barked wildly in the night. I jumped up. The tree above the leather lodge had been struck by lightning and caught fire. It was burning fast. The Captains, Charbonneau, and Sacagawea, holding Pomp, ran out of the lodge. We quickly pulled it away from the fire. Not a minute after, the top half of the tree, all aflame, crashed down in the spot where the lodge had stood. Were it not for the dog's warning, all inside would have been killed.

A terrible thing has happened! Seaman is near death.

Saint Peter shot a beaver. Seaman swam out to retrieve it, but the beaver was not badly wounded, and it put up a fight. Blood swirled in the water where the animals were struggling. At last Seaman managed to grab the beaver in his jaws and swim to shore. There he fell down, senseless. Capt. Lewis and I ran to him and found his hind leg was nearly cut in two where the beaver had bit him. Blood poured from the wound. Capt. Lewis bound his leg, but still it bled. The Captain says the bite cut an artery. He fears it will be fatal to his dog. Oh, Seaman, bright bounding spirit of our Adventure, we cannot lose you!

Above Sacagawea River
May 20, '05

Seaman lay at my feet in the white pirogue as we went. He was so very still, barely breathing. All day, I trickled water into his mouth, and rubbed his throat until he swallowed.

Capt. Lewis named a river flowing into the Missouri after Sacagawea. When Drewyer signed to tell her of this honor, she seemed puzzled.

Missouri River
May 21, '05

A violent storm raged all night, coating us with sand and grit. The wind blew so hard we could not light a fire, eat, nor sleep. The only one not bothered by the sandstorm was the dog, for I covered him head to tail with my blanket.

Missouri River
May 22, '05

Seaman laps water now. I chewed some meat until very tender and fed it to him. He got it down. Other than that, he never stirs nor opens his eyes. I am still greatly worried.

Missouri River
May 23, '05

Hard going today. The river here is shallow, so we had to pull the boats over many rocky patches with our elk-skin ropes. The sun beat down on us, making us sweat, which drew herds of mosquitoes. Sharp rocks in the river bottom poked holes in our moccasins.

Tonight we made ourselves new moccasins with double soles. Seaman lay beside me at the fire as I stitched. Colter came by, patted him, and the dog thumped his tail. A good sign!

Just before we turned in, I got out *Geography Made Easy* and looked at a drawing of a desert. It resembles the stretch where we are now, very dry with not much growing. Still, there is nothing easy about *this* geography.

Missouri River
May 26, '05

At last! We can see the mountains ahead. They are higher than I had expected. And covered with snow. The old trader never said a word to Capt. Lewis about that.

Seaman struggled to his feet tonight and gave himself a shake. All the men cheered him!

Missouri River
May 28, '05

Seaman walked a few steps but put no weight on his wounded leg. His appetite has returned. We all feed him scraps from our plates and spoil this much-loved member of our Corps.

Mouth of the Judith River
May 29, '05

Capt. Clark named a river for his sweetheart back home. This is the first we men had heard of her.

More trouble last night. As we lay sleeping, a large bull buffalo ran out of the river and stampeded helter-skelter through our camp. I heard a ruckus and barking and sat up in time to see Seaman rush out of the leather lodge and lunge at the buffalo, causing him to swerve. If the dog had not turned him, the buffalo would have trampled the lodge and all inside. At last the buffalo ran into the prairie and vanished, leaving us all half awake with our guns in hand.

Capt. Lewis stormed over to our guard, who turned out to be Charbonneau. The captain demanded to know why he never blew his horn. Charbonneau seemed to be saying that the bull galloped by so fast, he had no time to sound the alarm.

Colter said, "I think we are due another round of *boudin blanc*."

Seaman sat up in the boat all day. Chasing that buffalo seems to have done him good.

(Seaman)

Missouri River
May 30, '05

Tonight around the fire, Gibson said it nettles him how his feet freeze from standing in the icy water all day, hauling the boat, while at the same time, the hot sun burns the back of his neck to blisters.

Frazer said what nettles him are the slippery rocks in this stretch of the river. "And the pointed ones, too," he added, holding up the moccasin he was mending. It had several holes poked through its bottom.

Reuben Fields said what nettles him is seeing the

tall, snow-topped mountains ever before us and wondering how we will get over them.

Joseph Fields said it nettles him the way the river loops and bends back on itself like a writhing snake. He said, "What we could walk in an hour takes us a day by boat."

"Paddling against a dead hard wind nettles me," said Shields.

"Jumping into the river so many times a day to haul the boats over the shallows," said Whitehouse.

"Mosquitoes," said McNeal. "I am eaten alive."

"The elk-skin ropes," said Bratton. "When they're wet, they're slippery, hard to grip. And they're rotting."

"What nettles me," said York, "is how those ropes slice into my hands."

"Hands?" said Potts. "What about feet? Mine are bruised and bleeding."

"Treading on prickly pear cactuses is the worst," said Hall. "And plucking thorns out of my feet."

Collins said what nettled him was that his leather clothes were starting to smell mighty bad.

Colter said what nettled him was that Collins was starting to smell mighty bad.

We all broke up laughing then.

"What nettles you, Shannon?" Potts asked, and all eyes turned to me.

"Being hungry," I said, and they laughed again. "But," I added, "I would rather be hungry, frostbit, sunburned, and have my feet cut to ribbons than be in

187

Pittsburgh sorting nuts and bolts in a stuffy back room."

I was answered by a chorus of "Amen!" and "Yes, sir!"

We seem to feel some better tonight after airing our griefs.

Missouri River
May 31, '05

Another close call for the white pirogue! We stood waist-deep in the water, pulling her through a bad spot, when a rope broke. The boat swung around and banged into a cliff. Only by all of us working with every muscle we have did we manage to hold her until a new rope was tied on.

At noon, Capt. Lewis ordered us to pull over. He gave everyone a shot of whiskey. He is worried about us men, yet I think what nettles him most is the thought of losing his journals and Scientific Notebooks, where he has written down the temperature, the wind direction, and the exact measurements of every animal, plant, and mineral he has come across.

Tonight, after the fire burned down, Capt. Lewis had another dram of whiskey. He was as low as I have ever seen him.

"I fear that the white pirogue is haunted by an evil genie, Pup," he said. "The genie will not be happy until this boat and all it carries is sunk to the bottom of the river."

Capt. Lewis shot six elk today, which picked up his spirits. I am helping to scrape their hides. When we finish, we will roll them and store them in the barrel marked HIDES FOR THE IRON FRAME BOAT.

When Little Fox gave us directions, he never said how far away the landmarks were. I thought we would have come upon that tree with the eagle's nest long ago. We must have missed it. Now we are on the lookout for the Great Falls.

We are camped on a point of land where a large river flows into the river we are on, creating a fork. Which river is the Missouri? We cannot tell. Little Fox never said a word about a fork. The water flowing in from the north river is thick and muddy like the Missouri River. The river flowing in from the south is clear. The Captains think the clear river is the Missouri, but all of us men think it is the muddy river. Sgt. Pryor has gone up the north river to look for the Great Falls. Sgt. Gass has gone down the south river to do the same. The delay gives our feet a chance to mend.

Both sergeants came back. Neither found a waterfall. Most men are bedded down now. I am sitting up with Capt. Lewis while he frets.

"If we follow the wrong river, Pup, we may lose our chance to cross the mountains before winter," he said. "I fear this would badly discourage the Corps."

I answered him, "Can't you see by now that we men of the Corps of Discovery are not so easily discouraged?"

Unknown river from the south
June 4, '05

Capt. Lewis set out with a party this morning to explore the north river. I set out with Capt. Clark, Sgt. Gass, the Fields brothers, and York to follow the south river. We walked a long way along its clay banks, stomping on many a prickly pear. Rain pelted us. We were so glad when we stumbled across an old Indian lodge. We are sheltered there now, pulling prickers from our feet.

Unknown river from the south
June 6, '05

The rain turned the riverbank into a sticky, slippery mire. I lost my footing and fell so often I am bruised all over. This is the worst part of the trip yet. We trudged on and on but found no waterfall. Could Little Fox have been pulling our legs?

Fork of Two Rivers Camp
June 7, '05

Back at last! Capt. Lewis and his party are still out.

Fork of Two Rivers Camp
June 8, '05

Capt. Clark has been greatly worried about Capt. Lewis. Finally this evening he and his party straggled into camp, cold, wet, and exhausted. Their feet are shredded from the prickly pear. Seaman's paws are bloodied, too. They saw no sign of a waterfall. After all our pains, we still don't know which river to take.

Fork of Two Rivers Camp
June 11, '05

A dark mood has settled over Capt. Lewis. He stays in his tent, seeing no one.

Sacagawea has come down with a fever. As Capt.

Lewis is not up to it, Capt. Clark bled her.

Then Capt. Clark called us all together. "Whichever river we pick, we must travel fast and light to reach the mountains before winter," he said. "We will leave the red pirogue behind, hidden in the brush. We will travel on in the white pirogue and the canoes."

Capt. Clark gave out jobs. He asked Whitehouse and me if we would like to make a secret cache. We said we would. Only then did we discover that a cache is a great big hole dug in the earth for burying supplies too heavy to take along. And that we would do the digging.

Muscles ache from digging a great hole. Took all day. Other men carried the dirt we dug and threw it into the river. We lined our hole with dried sticks and grass. We put in the blacksmith bellows, hammers, and tongs, beaver traps, axes, kegs of corn, extra lead and gunpowder, and other heavy items. Then we shoveled dirt on top and set a plug of grass on top. No one seeing this spot would ever know it had been dug up.

Around the campfire tonight, Capt. Clark said he and Capt. Lewis believe the clear river flowing in from the south comes from the mountains and is the true Missouri River. Not one of us men agrees. Saint Peter, our Missouri River expert, said he would bet his fiddle on the north river.

When Capt. Clark retired to the leather lodge, Saint Peter brought out this same fiddle and we men danced and sang for hours. We all agree, without saying a word, that the Captains are our Captains, and where they lead, we will follow.

Fork of Two Rivers Camp
June 12, '05

Sacagawea is burning up with fever. Capt. Clark asked Collins and me to carry her into the shade, hoping to cool her. I sat with her awhile. At times she looked up, seeming to see fevered visions. She calls out to these phantoms. She is out of her head and far too sick to care for Pomp. Charbonneau is no help. He only cries and wails over his wife.

Capt. Clark has given me charge of the baby. Cannot write more now.

Pomp fell asleep in my arms by the fire. His mother is no better.

Capt. Clark says that tomorrow we will start up the southern river. Capt. Lewis and four men will travel ahead on land to hunt. I was glad to hear this plan, for Capt. Lewis is often revived by hunting.

Missouri (we hope) River
June 13, '05

Sacagawea is barely breathing. Capt. Clark put a poultice

of Peruvian bark on her belly, hoping to draw out the infection. York managed to feed her a small amount of his soup.

This morning I poured some of York's cooled soup into a rawhide funnel. I gave the small end to Pomp. He sucked eagerly, but when he discovered it was not his mother's milk, he set up a wail. Nothing could persuade him to take more.

I have seen Sacagawea put Pomp into his cradle board and swing it onto her back as easy as slipping on a shirt. Yet it took both Collins and Colter to get the baby cradled up and hitched on me.

We proceeded on. At first I had a hard time paddling with the baby on my back, but I got the hang of it. Rounding a bend, we found four butchered elk hanging from trees on the river bank. We stopped and cooked the meat on the spot. Thank you, Capt. Lewis and party!

Pomp takes little soup. He howls for milk. At last he had to be put to his poor mother's breast. Sick as she is, she wrapped her arms around him as he sucked.

Missouri River
June 14, '05

I am so afraid Sacagawea may die. Capt. Lewis brought her along to help bargain for horses with the Shoshone. But she has become an important member of our Expedition. All of us have come to count on her calming presence. The sight of her caring for her son has given our campsites a homey feel. Sacagawea has kept her head in times of danger and fed the whole Corps when game was scarce. She has had a hard life, but she is strong and has survived. I only hope she can pull through this sickness.

Joseph Fields came to our camp from Capt. Lewis's party. He says they have found the Great Falls. Right before it, they saw a tree with an eagle's nest, just as Little Fox said they would. The Captains were right. We are on the Missouri River after all!

Missouri River
June 16, '05

Capt. Lewis came to visit our party this afternoon. He is his old self again. He told us that Great Falls is not one waterfall. It is *five*. He has sent Sgts. Gass and Ordway to explore the falls and figure out the best way to carry our canoes around them. When Capt. Lewis heard that Sacagawea was still ill, he quickly went to her. He gave her some opium to help her sleep. Then he asked me to go to a sulfur spring he had seen on his way to our camp to fetch some water for Sacagawea. I put Pomp in the care of Colter and set off. I had not gone far when I heard Pomp shriek. I ran back, thinking to rescue the baby, but it turned out to be a shriek of joy. Colter was bouncing Pomp wildly up and down on his knee. Off I went to fetch the sulfur water.

Capt. Lewis said Sacagawea drank the sulfur water eagerly.

Sgts. Gass and Ordway have returned, looking grave. They measured the distance from the first fall to the fifth. It is a stretch of more than 18 miles! Worse, the surrounding hills are steep. And the woods are thick with trees and brush. They say we cannot carry our canoes over this land.

The Captains listened, nodding. Neither looked at all daunted. They huddled together for a few minutes.

Then Capt. Clark said, "We will hide the white pirogue here."

"We will proceed on in our small canoes," said Capt. Lewis. "And don't forget the iron-framed boat."

"But how will we carry our gear around the falls?" asked Whitehouse.

Capt. Lewis smiled. "We will build ourselves a truck."

Portage Camp, Missouri River
June 17, '05

Capt. Clark is overseeing the building of the truck. And the hauling of canoes and gear overland around the Great Falls. For this mission, he has set up a Portage Camp.

I am working on the truck. We cut down a large

cottonwood tree. Sgt. Gass and I sawed its wide trunk crosswise to make wheels. We made axles from the mast of the white pirogue.

This evening Sacagawea felt well enough to ask for Pomp. Tears of joy filled her eyes as I handed her the baby.

Hunting camp, Medicine River
June 19, '05

Sacagawea is tending Pomp again. I know he is glad, but I miss having him near me.

We have carried the iron rods of "The Experiment" some 3,000 miles by river from Pittsburgh. Now at last they will be put to use. Capt. Lewis has taken Shields, Joseph Fields, and Sgt. Gass to an island west of the Great Falls. He calls it White Bear Island, as he has seen several grizzlies. Why he has chosen a grizzly-infested island for his campsite, I cannot say, but this is where the four of them will put together the iron boat.

Before he left, Capt. Lewis named Drewyer, Reuben Fields, and me as hunters. He needs dozens more elk hides to cover his iron boat frame. No other hide will do. He ordered us to head up Medicine River and bring down as many elk as possible.

Evening: We shot seven deer.

***

Hunting camp, Medicine River
June 20, '05

Drewyer, Reuben, and I split up to increase our chances of finding more elk. I am now camped some 5 miles up Medicine River. So far I have shot three deer and two buffalo.

Hunting camp, Medicine River
June 23, '05

I heard whooping and hollering. I whooped and hollered back. Who should come striding into my camp but Capt. Lewis, Joseph Fields, and Seaman! The dog gave me a fine greeting. The Captain said he feared I was lost again, so he had paddled up the river to find me, but he said it in fun. He asked after the other hunters, but I do not know where they are camped.

Capt. Lewis tried to seem impressed by the seven deer and six buffalo I have shot so far. And by the hundreds of pounds of buffalo meat I have dried. Yet I could tell he was disappointed, for I have shot no elk.

This evening by the fire, the Captain told us that he had hoped to see more pitch pines in this region. He needs their sticky sap, called pitch, to seal the seams of the hides stitched together to cover his boat. This pitch will keep the seams from leaking.

***

Hunting camp, Medicine River
June 24, '05

This morning Capt. Lewis sent Joseph up the river to find his brother and Drewyer. The Captain will walk back to White Bear Island. He is eager to check on the progress of his boat. He asked me to load up his canoe with all my deer and buffalo meat and paddle down Medicine River to White Bear Island. Most likely the men portaging the boats and gear will be there by now. He expects they will be hungry.

White Bear Camp
June 25, '05

Oh, the portage is terrible! Whitehouse is sick with heatstroke. I sat with him while Capt. Lewis bled him. Afterward, Whitehouse told me the portage crew had endured prickly pear, swarms of mosquitoes, blazing heat, and pouring rain. After one rain, a huge herd of buffalo galloped by. Their hooves churned up the mud, and when it dried, the buffalo tracks hardened into sharp peaks. As the men walked over this stretch, the peaks stabbed through their moccasins and tore up their feet very bad. And yet, Whitehouse said, no one complains. They pull that wooden truck over the land by force of will. He showed me the palms of his hands. The skin is completely peeled away.

Capt. Lewis sits by the fire, stewing. Joseph Fields came back to report that neither Drewyer nor Reuben has shot any elk.

White Bear Camp
June 26, '05

The portaging men straggle into camp all day. Many are barefooted, as their moccasins gave out along the way. I am stitching new ones for them as fast as I can.

Mosquitoes very bad.

Capt. Lewis says we must travel lighter still. I am digging another cache. We will put in the blunderbusses and Capt. Lewis's writing desk.

What a surprise tonight! Capt. Lewis had us men sit while he gathered wood, hauled water, and cooked our supper. He boiled up enough dried buffalo meat to feed all the party. He made suet dumplings as a treat to thank us for working so hard.

White Bear Camp
June 28, '05

Grizzlies are everywhere. I sleep with my loaded rifle close at hand. Seaman patrols all night with whoever is on guard. When a grizzly approaches our camp, he barks wildly, trying to drive it away. By morning, the dog is so worn out he can barely keep his eyes open.

Capt. Lewis has given up on getting more elk to cover his iron boat. In addition to the twenty-eight elk hides he already has, he will use four buffalo hides. Shields singed the hair off these hides with a blazing torch and stunk up our camp something awful.

White Bear Camp
June 30, '05

No sleep. White Bears roaring all night long.

When I am not hunting, I help with the iron boat. Today I joined Frazer and Whitehouse in sewing together the scraped elk hides. We thread our needles with deer sinew.

Shields and Gass are sawing off tree limbs and shaving their bark. Reuben ties these limbs onto the boat frame as cross braces. The wood will help to keep the iron boat afloat. We can find no pine pitch, so Drewyer is cooking up a substitute. He boils down buffalo tallow and stirs in ground charcoal to make a tar. He hopes this tar will seal the seams of the stitched-together skins. While we work, Capt. Lewis rushes from man to man, supervising this project so dear to his heart. Colter and others have long made fun of this boat. Now no one says a word against it.

***

Capt. Clark, York, Charbonneau, and Sacagawea stumbled into camp this afternoon in an awful state. Capt. Clark told how, two days ago, they were walking to see the falls when a fierce storm struck. York had gone off to hunt buffalo. Capt. Clark pulled the others into a ravine to take shelter under a shelf of rock. Sacagawea took Pomp out of his cradle board. She unwrapped him, but before she could wrap him up again, the skies opened and a heavy rain poured down, sweeping all the baby's things away. Capt. Clark saw a great wave of water rushing toward them. He knew they would be drowned unless they got to higher ground. Charbonneau scrambled up out of the ravine. With Capt. Clark pushing from behind, Charbonneau pulled Sacagawea and Pomp to safety. Pomp's skin had become so slippery in the rain that Sacagawea could barely keep her grip on him. The water was waist high on Capt. Clark before he clambered up, saving himself just before a violent flood swept through the ravine. Capt. Clark, Charbonneau, and Sacagawea made their way out to the plain. There they found York frantically searching for them. He had thought to bring a canteen of rum and gave all a drink to warm them, even the baby.

Capt. Clark led the way back to Portage Camp. There they found the portage crew bleeding and in great confusion. During the storm, they had been caught out in the open. Once the rain let up, several of the men had stripped off their wet clothing, thinking to dry it.

Suddenly, hailstones the size of apples fell from the sky. The wind blew the stones at their bare bodies with awful force, knocking the men down. They left the truck on the plains and fled, injured and bleeding, back to Portage Camp. This is how Capt. Clark found them, poor men!

White Bear Camp
July 3, '05

Work on the iron boat is not going well. Every time we stick our needles through the hide, it makes a hole. The holes grow bigger as the hide shrinks back from the sinew thread. Drewyer's tar cannot plug these holes. Yet the Captain's hopes are high. He often says how light his boat is, how well designed.

The Captains gave us hunters leave to go and see the falls. Each fall was more magnificent than the one before. White spray leaps up from the water, catching the sunlight, making rainbows. The sheer force of the water rushing over the rocks roars louder than cannon fire. I have not seen any woolly mammoths, nor giant beavers, but the sight of these falls beats all.

On our way home, we shot several buffalo.

White Bear Camp
July 4, '05

The portage is over. It took us three weeks to carry the

canoes and gear over 18 rough miles.

Now we are all together again to celebrate our nation's 29th birthday. This evening, Capt. Lewis gave out the last of the whiskey. After we drank every last drop, Saint Peter played and we danced and sang until late, in spite of a roaring thunderstorm.

White Bear Camp
July 5, '05

The iron-framed boat is covered with hides. Today we turned her upside down on a scaffold and built small

Great

my hunting camp

Medicine River

Capt. Lewis's camp
(White Bear Island)

fires under her to dry the hides. They would dry, too, if only the rain would let up.

Capt. Clark's portage camp

Sulfur Springs

Portage Creek

Missouri River

Falls

Portage Trail

White Bear Camp
July 8, '05

Brushed on two coats of Drewyer's black tarry mix to make the boat watertight. Capt. Lewis cannot stop talking of the wonders of his craft. How she can be loaded with 4 tons of goods, yet she is so light she needs only five men to carry her over land.

Capt. Clark has gone off by himself, saying he wants to make some notes.

We packed our goods into the iron boat. We put in the seats. We fitted in the oars and shoved her into the river.

Capt. Lewis was delighted. "Ahhh!" he said. "She floats like a perfect cork!"

I asked Colter if he planned to boil his hat before he ate it.

We loaded up the canoes. We were ready to paddle off when a storm hit. Hard winds blew the rain sideways, wetting everything. We had no choice but to stop and unload the boats. When the storm passed, we discovered that the buffalo skins on the iron boat had held tight together, but the seams of the elk skin had come apart.

I have never seen a man as downcast as Capt. Lewis when he saw the leaky seams. He turned to face us men and said, "The boat will not serve."

Colter and I cut the skins off the iron frame and took the boat apart. We dug a cache and buried these heavy iron rods. We buried the truck wheels, too. Colter had it right about this boat all along. He will not have to eat his hat, but takes no pleasure in his prediction turning out to be true.

Canoe Camp
July 10, '05

I am with Capt. Clark's party. We spent the day chopping down cottonwoods and hollowing them out to make two new canoes.

When we set out this morning, Capt. Clark led us straight to a grove of large cottonwoods. (I wonder: Did he doubt Capt. Lewis's iron boat all along? If so, he never said a word.)

These new canoes must be bigger than the others. It will take the better part of a week for us to shape them. When they are finished, our party will head west in two large and six small canoes.

Canoe Camp
July 14, '05

We have finished the canoes. One is 25 feet long. The other is 33 feet. Some of the men are making seats and paddles. I specialize in poles.

Canoe Camp
July 15, '05

Even with the new canoes, we cannot fit all the gear and all the men into the boats, so we will take turns paddling and walking on shore.

We have seen no Indians since we left the Mandan. Capt. Lewis hopes to meet the Shoshone soon.

I am 18 today. I rarely feel like a pup now. To think it has been nearly two years since I first laid eyes on Capt. Lewis. How different my life would be had not that big shaggy dog of his jumped on me and knocked me down!

Missouri River
July 16, '05

This stretch of river is swift, narrow, and treacherous. Yet the shore is bright with flowers. Even the prickly pear, that devil to the feet of man, is pretty when blooming.

This afternoon we passed hills thick with pitch pines. I hoped Capt. Lewis would not see them, but of course he did. That man sees everything.

Gates of the Rocky Mountains
July 19, '05

Capt. Clark, York, Joseph Fields, and Potts have gone ahead looking for the Shoshone. The Captains fear that if a Shoshone scout were to spy us all together, he might think we are a war party and call his warriors to attack us. We are on alert.

The river here runs in a canyon between cliffs over 1,000 feet high. Capt. Lewis calls this place the Gates of the Rocky Mountains. It is a gloomy stretch. Except at midday, the sun is hidden behind a cliff. These cliffs come straight down to the river. There is no bank. Darkness fell tonight before we found a place fit for camping. When at last we pulled over, the site was filled with prickly pears. We could not find any wood, so had to make our cook fires with buffalo dung.

Tonight by the fire, I pulled seventeen prickly pear thorns from Seaman's footpads, poor dog.

Gates of the Rocky Mountains
July 20, '05

This morning a column of smoke rose out of the west. Capt. Lewis says the Shoshone may have set a fire as a signal to another band. We pulled over, placed a blanket on the narrow shore, and laid out trade items to show that we come in peace. We waited. No one came to us, so we got back into the boats and kept on. At every bend in the river we wonder: Are we paddling into a trap? We all feel anxious. Our spirits are low.

Gates of the Rocky Mountains
July 22, '05

Today, with Drewyer translating, Sacagawea told Capt.

Lewis that she knows this part of the river. Her people camped here in the summer when she was a girl. She says before long, we will reach Three Forks. This news gave us all a boost.

We have caught up with Capt. Clark. He has seen no Shoshone but had to stop walking because his poor feet are torn and bleeding from treading on prickly pear.

Gates of the Rocky Mountains
July 23, '05

Capt. Clark hobbled off again to look for the Shoshone. This man keeps going even in awful pain. The Fields brothers, Frazer, Drewyer, and Charbonneau went with him. The Captains brought Sacagawea all this way to speak with the Shoshone. Why did they not ask her to go along?

We hoisted American flags on our boats to show who we are. Then we set off.

Gates of the Rocky Mountains
July 24, '05

We passed a stretch of riverbank made of fine red clay. By signing, Sacagawea told us that her people come to this spot to collect red clay for painting their faces. Capt. Lewis ordered us to stop and get some of this red clay.

***

Current is so strong here we can hardly paddle. All of us are near exhaustion. This is the worst stretch of our journey. Poor Seaman! His paws look like pincushions, stuck with needle grass. Tonight I bathed his feet in cold water. I took out the needles. It was not easy, as they are barbed like tiny fishhooks.

I got Seaman's booties out of my pack, thinking they might protect his paws from stickers, but the dog ran from me when he saw them.

This morning we rounded a bend and found ourselves free of the towering cliffs. We saw a river rushing in from the southeast. A quarter mile farther on, two more rivers joined in. We have reached Three Forks! What a beautiful sight, these three rivers flowing gently through a wide stretch of plains and meadows into the Missouri River.

We proceeded on but stopped when we saw a note stuck on the branch of a young tree. It was from Capt. Clark. He wrote that we should make camp here at Three Forks and wait for him to return. We happily unpacked the canoes. We are so glad to rest.

Capt. Clark's party staggered into camp this afternoon. All were worn down, but the Captain was deathly pale. He fell to his knees, vomiting. Several of us ran to help him. When we had propped him up by the fire, he told us he suffers from fever, chills, boils, infected mosquito bites, and a stoppage of the bowels. Yet he marched 16 miles this day to reach us. Capt. Lewis took off Capt. Clark's bloody moccasins. He soaked his feet in warm water and recommended a dozen Thunder Clappers. Capt. Clark agreed to take five.

This evening I walked with Capt. Lewis. He talked of nothing but finding the Shoshone.

"We need horses, Pup," he said. "We need to get over the mountains before winter. We need game. The Shoshone have horses. They know the best place to cross the mountains. They know where we can find game. We must find the Shoshone soon, or our Expedition will fail."

He sounded so terrible gloomy, I did not know what to say.

Three Forks
July 29, '05

My spirits are much improved by these days of rest. All the men seem revived.

Collins and I gathered boughs to make a shady bower for Capt. Clark. We helped him lie down beneath it so as to cool his fever. The boil on his ankle looks red, swollen, and painful.

This afternoon, Capt. Lewis asked me to take notes while he spoke with Sacagawea. With Drewyer interpreting, he asked her to tell him the Shoshone term for white man. Sacagawea went back and forth with Drewyer. Several times she shook her head. She seemed to be saying that her people had never seen a white man, so they had no word for such. Yet Capt. Lewis kept asking. At last Sacagawea came up with a term. I wrote it down the way it sounded: *tab-ba-BONE*. Capt. Lewis said it over and over, seeming pleased.

The Captain left. Sacagawea signed some more with Drewyer. Later, he told me she had said it was here at Three Forks that Horned Weasel and his Hidatsa raiding party had captured her and Otter Woman. She said a third Shoshone girl was with them. She saw the attackers and quickly leaped through the river to the shore and ran, yet Sacagawea doubts that she got away. She believes that most of her people were killed in the raid.

Jefferson River
Aug. 3, '05

Capt. Lewis and a party, including Sacagawea, have gone up the north river on foot, seeking the Shoshone. The Captain named this river the Jefferson.

I am with Capt. Clark's party, following behind them, dragging the canoes through the shallow waters of the Jefferson. The riverbank is full of deep, dangerous holes. The prairie is covered with prickly pears and dense willow thickets. We had to hack our way through them to make any progress. Every which way, the going is hard.

We reached another river flowing into the Jefferson, but found no note from Capt. Lewis telling us which fork he took. Capt. Clark has decided we should take the north fork, which he named the Wisdom River.

Late morning, Capt. Clark sent me ahead on the Wisdom to hunt. I went alone, for all others are needed to drag the canoes. After hunting, I am to make camp beside the river and wait for the rest of the party to catch up to me. Not much game here. Had no luck today.

Got one deer. Game is scarce, but mosquitoes are not. Neither are large, black biting flies. Herds of small green flies also swarm around my head. I am deeply grateful there are no eye gnats.

Got two more deer. Have gutted all three and cut up the meat to dry. Am scraping the hides. They will quickly be used for new moccasins.

***

Rain, thunder, and lightning. I thought Capt. Clark and the men would have reached me by now. If they do not show by tomorrow morning, I will walk back down the river to meet them.

I am reminded of being separated from the party last year. This time I have plenty of powder and balls. I have three deer to keep me fed. Still, I will be glad to reach my Corps.

No sign of the others. I hung the meat in trees and walked up the river a stretch. I thought somehow the party might have got ahead of me. Yet the river here is hardly more than a trickle. The men could not have dragged the boats up it.

I returned to my camp. With the hides I rigged up a sling arrangement for carrying the meat. I will drag it behind me as I go.

I am standing where the Jefferson River forked. Where I left Capt. Clark and the others. No one is here. I hollered some. No one hollered back. I am itching to fire off my gun as a signal, but I do not want to alarm any Shoshone who might be around. All I can figure is

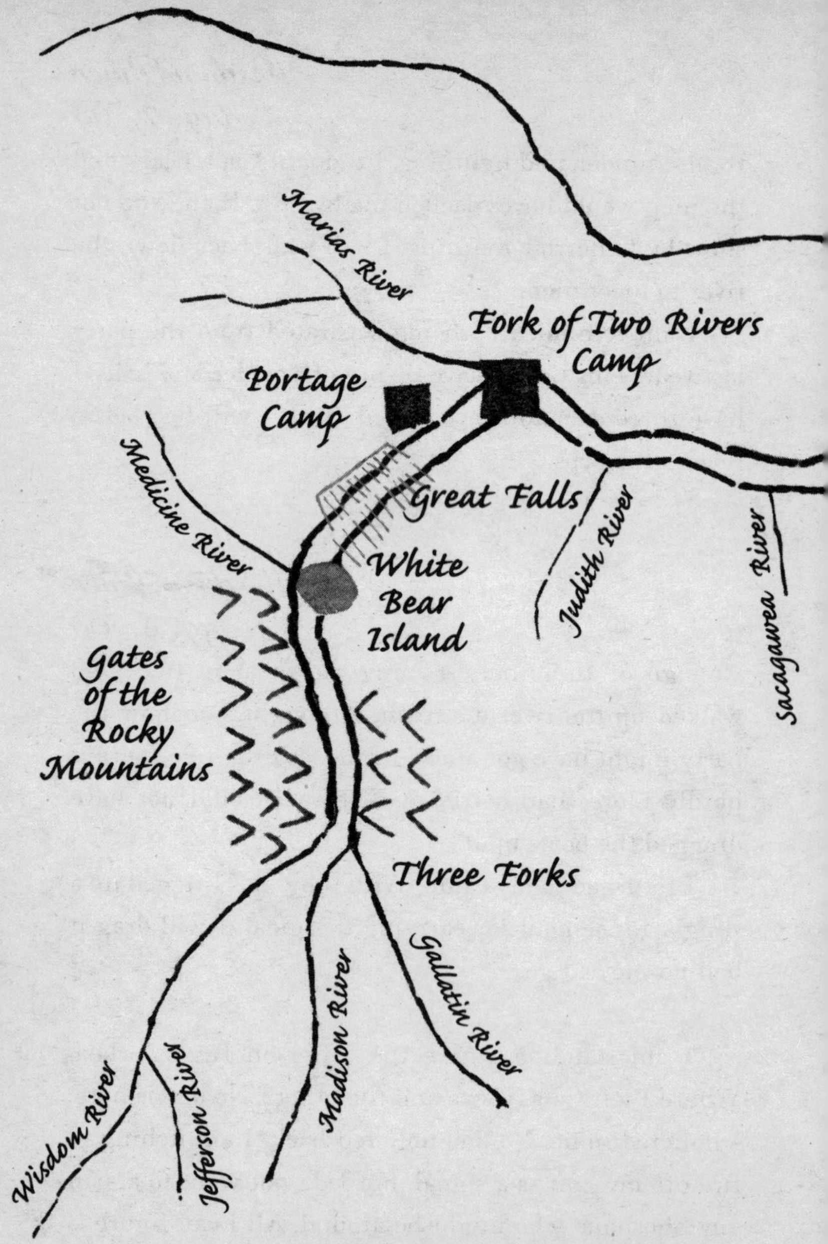
Marias River
Fork of Two Rivers Camp
Portage Camp
Medicine River
Great Falls
Judith River
Sacagawea River
White Bear Island
Gates of the Rocky Mountains
Three Forks
Gallatin River
Madison River
Jefferson River
Wisdom River

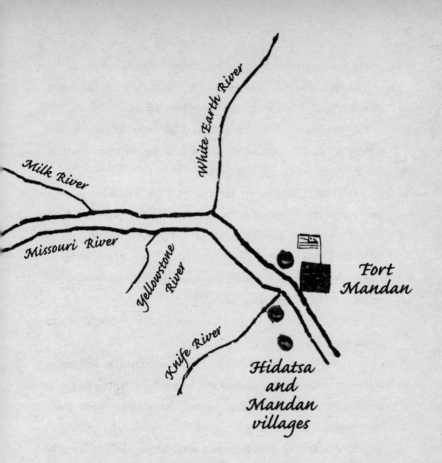

Milk River

White Earth River

Missouri River

Yellowstone River

Knife River

Fort Mandan

Hidatsa
and
Mandan
villages

that the party must have gone up the south fork. I will
sleep here tonight and go up it myself tomorrow.

Jefferson River, south fork
Aug. 9, '05

I came upon my party breaking camp this morning.

Collins called out, "Here is our lost pup!"

I had deerskins slung over my shoulder. I was lugging meat. This was a far cry from the last time my

party found me, sitting by the river, so low in spirit.

Colter offered to braid some elk hide to make me a harness and leash so I won't get lost again.

I answered, "If the party will only let me know when it plans to pull up stakes and set off up another river, I will be much obliged."

Whitehouse told me that Capt. Lewis had left a note for our party where the two rivers flowed together. The note told us to take the south fork. Capt. Lewis stuck the note on a young tree. The Captains figure a beaver must have come along, gnawed the tree down, and swum off with it to his dam, note and all.

Capt. Lewis called to Drewyer and Shields to ready their packs.

"I want you men to come with me up the Jefferson River to look for the Shoshone," he said. Then the Captain eyed me. "Your feet are in better shape than most, Pup. You come, too."

The Captain put Seaman in Hugh McNeal's care, then we four took off in search of the Shoshone. We marched 16 miles today, but saw no sign of any Indian.

Rattlesnake Cliffs
Aug. 10, '05

Set off early, following an Indian trail beside the Jefferson River toward the mountains. Drewyer went off to hunt. Capt. Lewis led the others of us under a high rocky cliff to shelter from rain and hailstones. Drewyer returned

with deer meat. We kindled a fire and cooked it. As we ate,
I spied six rattlers.

We set off again following the river for some miles
until we reached a plain where it forked in two. Capt.
Clark would have no way of knowing which fork we
took, so Capt. Lewis asked me to write him a letter saying to make camp at this fork until we come back. I
wrote: "Wait here until we return." Then I found a dry
willow branch. I whittled it into a pole, pounded it into
the ground near the fork, and fastened the letter to it. I
figure a dry pole is of no interest to any beaver.

No sign of the Shoshone.

Jefferson River
Aug. 11, '05

We have lost the Indian trail. Capt. Lewis said we
must spread out as we walk across the valley to look
for it. Drewyer was to walk to the north, Shields to the
south, and Capt. Lewis between them. I was to stick by
the Captain.

"If you see the trail again or want the others to stop,
put your hat on the muzzle of your gun," Capt. Lewis
told us. "Raise your gun high in the air so that the others can see the hat and know it for a signal."

We took off walking. After an hour or so, I spied a
man on horseback in the distance. I pointed. Capt. Lewis
stopped. He put his scope to his eye.

"It is a brave, riding bareback," Capt. Lewis

said, keeping his voice low.

I saw that the brave carried a bow and a quiver of arrows. His horse was very fine. His dress was different from any Indian we had seen.

"At last," the Captain whispered. "Shoshone."

Capt. Lewis and I kept walking toward the brave. He continued riding toward us. When we were some 200 feet apart, the brave stopped. We stopped, too. All was still.

Moving with great care so as not to startle the Indian, Capt. Lewis took a blanket from his pack. He held it by two corners. He waved it over his head three times, then spread it on the ground, as he had heard that this is a sign of friendship. The brave stayed where he was, not seeming to recognize this sign. He began to look from side to side. Had he caught sight of Shields and Drewyer? I turned and saw that the two were still walking toward him. Capt. Lewis muttered that he wished the men would stop, but he dared not yell nor give the hat signal, for fear of frightening the brave away.

The Captain told me to lay trinkets on the blanket to show that we come in peace. I put out mirrors, beads, a jar of face paint, a small American flag. The brave stayed still. I doubted that he could see the small objects at such a distance.

Moving slowly, Capt. Lewis handed me his rifle. Unarmed, he began to walk at a snail's pace toward the brave. The Indian watched. Capt. Lewis drew closer. The rider turned his horse as if ready to flee. This was the last thing Capt. Lewis wanted. He cried out the word Sacagawea had given him for white man, *"Tab-ba-bone! Tab-ba-bone!"* He called it loudly, over and over. The brave stared at Capt. Lewis. Then his eyes darted from Shields to Drewyer and back again. They were still advancing. Capt. Lewis was at his wit's end. He grabbed his gun back from me. He put his hat on the muzzle and raised it over his head. I wondered, what did the brave make of this strange act?

Drewyer saw the signal. He stopped.

But Shields's eyes were fastened on the Indian. On he went.

Capt. Lewis lowered his gun. He held up more trinkets. Again he cried, *"Tab-ba-bone!"*

When this had no effect, the Captain rushed forward, shoving up the sleeves of his shirt as he ran. I figured he was trying to show the rider the pale color of the skin on his arms, as that on his face and hands was deeply browned by the sun. This behavior seemed to startle the brave as nothing had done before. He quickly turned his horse, gave it a kick, and galloped away.

I will not dwell on the tongue-lashing Capt. Lewis meted out to Shields, and even to Drewyer. The men did not enjoy it.

Capt. Lewis had me cut a young tree and strip the bark off to make a pole. He attached a small American flag to this pole and ordered me to carry the stars and stripes as we followed the tracks of the Indian horse. Capt. Lewis is worried that the brave will ride back and warn his people. He fears that any minute a Shoshone war party may ride out to attack us.

We followed the horse's tracks until a storm came on and washed them out. We made camp. We are wet, miserable, and have little to eat for supper.

Headwaters of the Missouri River
Aug. 12, '05

On edge all night. Ate the last of our deer meat this morning. We have pork scraps, but we are saving them.

Walked some 4 miles up a gentle slope beside the river, which is hardly more than a stream now. It grew narrower and narrower, and at last it was so small that I planted one foot on the left bank and the other foot on the right. I raised the flag high over my head and said, "I have traveled up the whole length of the Missouri River and lived to bestride her!"

The other men chuckled at this performance. Then Shields outdid me by passing a stream of his own water across the river.

We followed what was left of the river to a bubbling spring. We had reached the very beginning of the Missouri River! I felt awed standing at the site we had traveled so long and hard to find. We each bent down in turn and took a drink of its pure, cold waters.

Capt. Lewis grew excited. He said the ridge right above us marked the end of Louisiana Territory. To the west lie lands unclaimed by any nation—Parts

Unknown. Capt. Lewis called the ridge the "backbone of our continent." Rivers that begin east of this point, such as the Missouri, flow east. Rivers that begin west of this ridge flow west. We felt happy to think that from here on out, we will be paddling downstream.

We climbed up to the ridge then, eager to drink from the source of the great westward-flowing Columbia River. Yet when we reached the top and looked out, we saw only steep, craggy hills. And beyond the hills rose up not a narrow ridge of mountains, but a wide range of mountains so vast they took my breath away. Gigantic mountains. Rocky Mountains. Shining Mountains, their tops glistening with snow. Mountains that went on and on and *on*! Mountains way beyond anything I had ever imagined.

Nowhere did we see any sign of the wide, westward-flowing Columbia River that President Jefferson had been so sure we would find.

I glanced at Capt. Lewis. Before him was a sight that put an end to his dream of discovering a Northwest Passage. I feared a dark mood might overtake him. The Captain stared at the sight before him for some time. Then he turned to me and said, "One way or another, we must get ourselves across these mountains. Are we up to it, Pup?"

I looked out at the immense mountains. I looked back at my Captain.

"Yes, sir," I told him. *"Yes, sir!"*

***

After we ate our pork-scrap meal, we scrambled down the steep, west side of the ridge. About a mile on we found a clear, swift stream that Capt. Lewis believes is the beginning of the Columbia, and we had ourselves a drink. We proceeded on 10 miles and made camp.

I took *Geography Made Easy* from my pack. I showed the Captain and the others page 43, where the Rocky Mountains are drawn as a single chain of mountains. This simple picture looks nothing like the mountains that rise up ahead of us, seeming never to end. Page 58 shows the area between the Rocky Mountains and the Pacific Ocean—Parts Unknown—to be one large and empty space.

"Now we will fill it in!" said Capt. Lewis.

Shoshone village, Lemhi River
Aug. 13, '05

This morning, on an empty belly, I picked up the flag and we set off. After some miles, we came upon a Shoshone man and two women with their dogs. Capt. Lewis quickly took the flag from me. He hurried toward them, waving it and calling, *"Tab-ba-bone! Tab-ba-bone!"* The Indians took flight. Their dogs scampered after them.

Capt. Lewis called to me, "Run, Pup! Catch one of the dogs."

I gave chase, but the dogs ran swifter. On going back to Capt. Lewis, I discovered that, had I caught a dog, he hoped to tie a kerchief loaded up with beads and trinkets around its neck, then send it back to its masters, bearing our friendly gifts.

Now Capt. Lewis is more worried than ever that these Indians will cause a war party to come and attack us. Still, we pressed on. We climbed a hill, and at its peak, we nearly stumbled over three Shoshone women. One about Sacagawea's age quickly sprinted off, but an old woman and a young girl sat where they were, their heads bowed, as if waiting for us to kill them or take them prisoner. Capt. Lewis handed me his gun. He grabbed his pack and started toward the pair, with many a *tab-ba-bone*! When he reached them, he rolled up his sleeve to show his fair skin. The woman and girl only clung to each other, terrified. Capt. Lewis opened his pack and took out beads and a mirror. The Shoshone shrank back from him. Then he took out some red clay from the riverbank. Seeing this clay, the old woman smiled. Because we had red clay, at last she seemed to understand that we meant her no harm. Once more, Sacagawea had helped us.

Capt. Lewis beckoned us men to come forward. Drewyer signed with the woman, asking her to call back the girl who had run off. The Captain did not want her to alert any Shoshone warriors. The woman called, and before long the girl came out from her hiding place.

Pleased, Capt. Lewis gave more trinkets to the woman and girls. He streaked their faces with red paint. Then he asked the woman to lead us back to her people. He said he wished to speak with the chief. Drewyer signed this message. The woman nodded. She and the girls began walking, and we four followed.

We had not gone far when pounding hooves sounded. I looked up. A large band of Shoshone warriors came galloping toward us! The men carried bows and arrows. A few had rifles. We froze where we were. I thought they would trample us, but just before they reached us, their leader called a halt. All quickly reined in their ponies.

The woman hurried over to the man who led the party. Capt. Lewis quickly laid his rifle on the ground. He told us men to stay put, and he followed her. As she spoke, the woman held up the mirror and beads Capt. Lewis had given her. The chief listened. He looked at Capt. Lewis. Then he jumped down from his horse.

I tightened my finger on the trigger of my gun. We were outnumbered, but I would not let my Captain be murdered where he stood. I would die shooting first.

I watched warily as the chief put his arms around Capt. Lewis. He gave him something of a bear hug. He pressed his cheek to the Captain's cheek. Over and over he said what sounded like *"Ah-hi-e."* I let go of the trigger.

A warrior sprang from his pony. He ran to me. He opened his arms and hugged me to his bosom. When this hug ended, another warrior stood waiting to do the same. And then another. The whole troop hugged each of us in turn. When at last the embracing ended, our faces were streaked with paint. Never did I imagine our meeting with the Shoshone would begin with such a hearty welcome!

The Shoshone took off their moccasins. We did the

same. Then we all sat down in a circle and smoked a pipe of peace. Capt. Lewis gave the chief an American flag. Drewyer says his name is Cameahwait. He does not know what this might mean in English.

We followed on foot as the Shoshone rode back to their village on the Lemhi River. When we arrived, Capt. Lewis smiled as he eyed a pen holding many fine horses.

The Shoshone villagers were lean and looked hungry. They stared at us as we walked by. I remembered Sacagawea saying they had never seen white men. Drewyer was able to sign with one of them. He discovered that in English *tab-ba-bone* means something close to "stranger."

Only one tepee stood in the village. Drewyer told us that all the others had been destroyed in a recent raid by the Blackfeet. We were invited inside and seated ourselves upon evergreen boughs covered over with antelope hide. Again we smoked. Capt. Lewis gave out his few remaining gifts.

We had not eaten in a full day, so I was glad to hear Capt. Lewis ask Drewyer to let Cameahwait know that we were hungry. When the chief understood, he looked downcast. He told Drewyer that his people were near to starving. He said if the Shoshone had rifles, they would no longer have to hide in the mountains for fear of their enemy, the Blackfeet. If they had rifles, they could camp in the plains all summer long, hunting buffalo. Capt. Lewis had to tell the chief that our party is not trading in guns. But he promised that other Americans would come soon, bringing guns for the Shoshone.

Cameahwait nodded. Then he called out, asking his people to bring us some of what little food they had. They brought cakes mixed with wild berries. Our hunger turned it into a fine meal.

Afterward, Capt. Lewis asked Drewyer to sign that one of their own people was with our larger party, but this proved too much for his signs. He was able to ask the chief whether we might paddle canoes down a nearby river to the Columbia. The chief shook his head. He said this river is too narrow for travel. Then he added something worse. He said the Shoshone never travel west. There are no buffalo in the west. And from here, it is too difficult to cross the Shining Mountains.

As we left the tepee, I expected Capt. Lewis to begin muttering. But all he said was, "Maybe Cameahwait is not telling us the whole story."

Shoshone village, Lemhi River
Aug. 14, '05

Capt. Lewis turned in early last night, but Drewyer, Shields, and I stayed up and danced with the Shoshone until dawn.

The Shoshone dressed for the dance in deerskin, decked out with beads and shells or robes made with the fur of wolves and buffalo. Some men draped tippets around their shoulders. These are otter or ermine pelts with the head, feet, and tails still attached. Some had on leggings decorated up the sides with what I took to be the black-haired tails of some sort of antelope. But when I looked closer, I saw that the trim was not fur, but hair dangling down from shriveled human scalps.

This morning Drewyer stayed with Capt. Lewis to translate. Some braves invited Shields and me to go hunting. We said yes, yet kept our guard up, as we do not want to end up decorating a pair of Shoshone leggings.

The braves lent us ponies but they had no saddles. Shields and I mounted up. Gripping our ponies' sides tightly with our knees, we galloped after the Shoshone. They make riding bareback look easy. It is not. When we spotted a herd of antelope, the braves, still galloping, put arrows to their bows and shot. Shields and I could not quite get the hang of aiming our rifles while being jolted about on the back of a horse. In the end, we reined in our ponies and let the braves gallop off after the herd. An hour later, they came back without any game. Shields and I marched off on our own then, determined to impress our hosts by shooting something to eat, but we, too, returned empty handed.

Back at the village, we found Capt. Lewis and Drewyer talking with the Shoshone chief.

"Cameahwait, we would be grateful if you would have your people bring thirty horses and come with us to our camp," Capt. Lewis was saying. "We will load our gear onto these horses and travel back here so that we might trade with you for horses for our journey over the mountains."

When Drewyer translated this, Cameahwait shook his head. "My people need meat," he replied. "This is their time to go east to the plains to hunt buffalo."

Capt. Lewis asked again for Cameahwait's help. And again. And again. At last the chief was worn down by our Captain. He promised that he and his people will help us.

Shoshone village, Lemhi River
Aug. 15, '05

Awoke hungry as a wolf. I made us a breakfast of flour cakes with berries and took some to Chief Cameahwait. He was thankful.

We packed up, ready to march back to the fork in the river where Capt. Clark would be camped, waiting for us. None of the Shoshone got ready to go with us. By way of Drewyer, Capt. Lewis asked Cameahwait what was wrong. The chief looked uneasy. At last he said his braves believe that we are in league with their enemy, the Blackfeet. They fear that our real purpose is to lead them into an ambush. Capt. Lewis begged the chief to tell the braves that this was not true. He did so, but still the warriors refused to go.

Capt. Lewis grew desperate. He said, "I thought the Shoshone were brave men. Are they so afraid to die?"

When Drewyer told this to the chief, Cameahwait drew himself up tall and said he was not afraid to die. He mounted his horse. He called to his braves that he was going with us. Six of his warriors mounted up as well. Capt. Lewis told us men to start marching. The chief and the six braves rode after us. More braves jumped on their horses then and came, too. Three squaws followed on foot. In the end, sixteen Shoshone came with us to meet Capt. Clark.

Camped for the night. No luck hunting, so we cooked up the little flour that was left, sharing it with Cameahwait and one brave. The rest of the Shoshone had nothing to eat.

Shoshone territory,
heading east over Lemhi Pass
Aug. 16, '05

Capt. Lewis asked Drewyer to sign to Cameahwait that he and Shields were going hunting. He asked Cameahwait not to send any of his braves with them, as too many hunters might scare away the game.

Hearing this, Cameahwait grew alarmed. He seemed to think that Drewyer and Shields might be sneaking off to meet the Blackfeet. When the men left, the chief sent braves to follow them.

I am in camp with Capt. Lewis. I try to keep busy writing in this journal or copying out pages for the Captain. I try not to worry over Drewyer and Shields. Yet what if, by chance, there are Blackfeet nearby? The Shoshone will think we are in cahoots with them.

A Shoshone warrior came galloping into camp. Capt. Lewis and I grabbed our guns and leaped up. The warrior jumped from his horse. He spoke excitedly to Cameahwait. What was he saying? It was some moments before we understood his news: Drewyer had shot a deer.

In an instant, every warrior in camp sprang onto his horse. Two riders circled Capt. Lewis and me, motioning for us to jump on in front of them, which we did. Off we galloped at full speed. I gripped that pony's neck so tight I feared I might strangle him.

By the time we reached Drewyer, he had cleaned the deer and sat roasting a hindquarter over a fire. He had tossed aside the innards—kidney, liver, intestines, and such. The starving Shoshone leaped from their horses and ran to these unused parts and began stuffing them into their mouths. Blood streamed down their chins and arms. Seeing this, Capt. Lewis gave the rest of the deer meat to Cameahwait. He and his braves did not wait to roast it but quickly ate it raw. The four of us dug into the roasted hindquarter. It tasted better than any feast.

This afternoon, Drewyer and Shields brought in two more deer and an antelope. We men and the Shoshone all ate our fill.

We traveled on toward the fork. Capt. Lewis told Cameahwait that before long, we would reach Capt. Clark's camp. To our surprise, Cameahwait reined in his horse and jumped off. His men did the same. What were they doing?

Cameahwait walked up to one of his warriors. He said a few words. The warrior took off his tippet and gave it to the chief. In this way, the chief collected three more tippets. Now Cameahwait stepped up to Capt. Lewis. He put a tippet around his shoulders. Shields, Drewyer, and I got decorated the same way. I understood. We men were deeply tanned. With tippets around our shoulders, we looked like Shoshone. If we led Cameahwait and his men into an ambush, the Blackfeet would think we were Shoshone and kill us, too.

Capt. Lewis eagerly entered into the spirit of the exchange. He took off his Captain's hat and gave it to Cameahwait. He motioned to us men to do the same with our hats. I obeyed, but not so eagerly. What if there were Blackfeet around?

We proceeded on, a Shoshone warrior leading the way, carrying a United States flag.

We rounded a bend. In the distance, I spied the fork where I had left the note for Capt. Clark, telling him to wait there until we returned. I expected to see our little fleet of boats in the river, but there were no boats. There was no sign of Capt. Clark or the men or a camp. Cameahwait and his men looked at us with suspicion. They began to grumble. They huddled together, talking low.

Just as I thought things could not get worse, Capt. Lewis strode over to Cameahwait and handed the chief his rifle. He motioned to us men to give our guns to the braves. It was not easy to let go of the only thing that might save me in a pinch. Yet I obeyed. And there we stood, surrounded and outnumbered by Shoshone braves armed with our own rifles.

By way of Drewyer, Capt. Lewis told Cameahwait that if our party was leading them into an enemy ambush, they could shoot us. Cameahwait nodded. He seemed to mean that he *would* shoot us. How I hoped that all the Blackfeet on this earth were miles off in the prairie, hunting buffalo.

Our situation was very bad. Keeping his voice low, Capt. Lewis leaned toward me and said, "That note you wrote to Capt. Clark may help us now, Pup."

Then, with Drewyer signing, Capt. Lewis said, "Chief Cameahwait, Capt. Clark most likely left a note at the fork in the river, telling us where to find him. Let us send one of your men and one of my men to fetch it."

The chief nodded. Drewyer and a warrior were quickly dispatched to get the note. Capt. Lewis seemed confident, but I was not so sure. I had left that note days ago. Would it still be there? What if beavers liked dry willow branches after all?

At last the men returned. The warrior waved the note, speaking to Cameahwait. He must have said that Drewyer found it on a branch by the river. The chief gave the note to Capt. Lewis. The Captain knew what it said, of course: "Wait here until we return." That is what he had told me to write. Yet now he looked at the note and said aloud, as though reading, words he hoped might soon prove true. "Capt. Lewis, we have taken the boats and gone to hunt. We will come back up the river soon. Signed, Captain William Clark."

Drewyer translated what the Captain had pretended to read. Cameahwait listened. Then he agreed to wait here until Capt. Clark arrives. Yet he does not look pleased. Neither do his braves.

Still waiting. The Shoshone hold our rifles. They are nervous. Every sound makes them jump. If Capt. Clark does not come soon, I think we will be shot.

Camp at fork of river
Aug. 17, '05

Capt. Lewis fretted through the night. This morning he told Cameahwait that they should each send a scout to see if Capt. Clark is coming. The chief agreed, and Drewyer and a brave set off.

Now the Captain, Shields, and I are waiting, all in ill spirits.

How our spirits soared when Drewyer marched into camp followed by Capt. Clark. (In fact, he *had* taken the party down the river to hunt.) Charbonneau, Sacagawea, and Pomp came with him. When I saw them, I let out such a whoop!

Cameahwait hugged Capt. Clark. The warriors hugged him. His red hair was a source of great amazement to them, and they began stringing shells into it. Capt. Clark did not appear to mind this attention.

When it seemed that all was peaceful, Capt. Lewis,

Drewyer, Shields, and I took off the tippets and returned them to their owners. We got our hats and rifles back. A moment later, the rest of our party marched into camp. If they had seen us without our guns, we never would have heard the end of it.

When York strode into camp, the Shoshone quickly abandoned Capt. Clark and gathered around him. Once more he put up with having his skin rubbed and his hair touched. York seemed glad when Hugh McNeal arrived with Seaman, and the Shoshone left him to run over and admire our dog. Before long, his fur was decorated with braids, shells, and beads.

All this while, Sacagawea was walking among her own people, speaking her own tongue, her face filled with joy. I thought she must be telling them who she was, how she had been taken in a Hidatsa raid. The three Shoshone women who had come with us were gathered round her, admiring Pomp and stroking his head. Suddenly one of the women gasped and burst out crying. Sacagawea, too, began to weep. The women embraced each other, sobbing. Drewyer says he believes this woman is Sacagawea's girl-hood friend, the one who ran through the river fleeing the Hidatsa raiders. Later we discovered that this was true. She is now called Jumping Fish in honor of her escape.

We set up camp by our boats near the fork of the rivers, then Capt. Lewis invited the Shoshone to a council. We privates went to work hammering stakes into the ground and attaching our sail to serve as a canopy. We put on our dress uniforms and stood at attention as Cameahwait and other Shoshone arrived.

Capt. Lewis decided that sign language would not do for the sort of talk he had in mind, so he set up a chain of translation. Cameahwait would speak Shoshone to Sacagawea. Sacagawea would give his words in Hidatsa to Charbonneau. He, in turn, would give the message to Labiche in French, and Labiche would give it to Capt. Lewis in English.

Drewyer's nose got bent out of joint at not being part of the chain, but he signed to the Shoshone to explain how the talks would work. When Cameahwait understood, he began to speak. He had said only a few words when Sacagawea gave a loud cry. I was jolted by this behavior, as Sacagawea is always calm and quiet. Yet now she ran to Cameahwait and threw her arms around his neck. Tears streamed down her cheeks. She began talking very fast as she unwrapped the blanket she wore and tried to throw it over Cameahwait's head. I feared she was fevered again and out of her mind. Capt. Clark stepped forward. He began pulling Sacagawea away, when suddenly Cameahwait reached out and embraced her with great emotion. It took some time, but at last we were led to understand that Cameahwait is Sacagawea's older brother. Each had thought the other long dead. I was near to tears myself, watching those two cling to each other and weep.

Capt. Lewis is in the highest of spirits. He has delayed the council to give sister and brother time to speak in private, which I believe is what Sacagawea was trying to do when she threw her blanket over her brother's head.

Sacagawea has brought us more good fortune. Now surely the Shoshone will trust us.

Council started up again. Through the translation chain, Capt. Lewis asked Cameahwait to gather as many horses as necessary to transport our goods over the Lemhi Pass, and to their village on the Lemhi River where we could trade for some horses. Cameahwait replied that he did not have enough horses to trade to us, but he would return to his village and ask his people to come and help us over the pass.

That business accomplished, Capt. Lewis began giving gifts. He gave Cameahwait a large peace medal, a uniform coat, and trousers. He asked Cameahwait to identify the lesser chiefs. Cameahwait pointed out two men. The Captain gave them smaller medals, shirts, and leggings, but they seemed to feel shortchanged. Capt. Clark saw this. After the council, he asked York to give these chiefs two of his own uniform coats. This pleased them. Through Drewyer, Capt. Clark told them that after they help us over the pass, he will give them more gifts.

The council ended when Colter and Collins came in with game. We roasted it and feasted with the Shoshone.

Camp Fortunate
Aug. 18, '05

Capt. Lewis named this place Camp Fortunate, as we are so lucky to have held out until Capt. Clark arrived.

Other bands of Shoshone are gathering nearby so they can all go east to hunt buffalo together. Capt. Lewis managed to trade some of our goods for three of their horses. Unknown to the Captains, Colter made a trade as well. For a knife and his uniform shirt and trousers, he got himself a pony.

"The next time the Corps puts on a dress parade," Colter said, "I'll have to watch."

Sacagawea looks so happy. She, Pomp, and Charbonneau are going to the Shoshone village with Cameahwait. They will bring people back to our camp to help us carry our goods.

I am making wooden pack saddles for the horses. Others are cutting leather thongs to bind these saddles tightly to the backs of the horses for our trip over the Shining Mountains.

Yesterday was Capt. Lewis's 31st birthday. No one thought to mention it. Today the Captain is in one of his dark moods. I think it best not to bring it up.

We are making piles of items too heavy to carry over the mountains. After dark, some of us will go off to a spot that is secret from the Shoshone and dig another cache. I will add one personal item: *Geography Made Easy*.

Cameahwait, Sacagawea, Charbonneau, and dozens of Shoshone rode into Camp Fortunate today. Sacagawea wore a wide belt made entirely of blue beads, the color most prized by all native peoples. Other Shoshone wore clothing decorated with porcupine quills dyed different colors. They wore earrings with clusters of beads and shells. Some braves had painted their faces red. Some had painted their horses red and strung bird feathers into their tails. A few braves wore brown bear claw collars ornamented with beads. (Yet none compare to Colter's grizzly claw necklace.)

The Shoshone looked hungry. Capt. Lewis asked us to make a meal for them with what we had, which was fish, corn, and beans. We did this, and the people were so glad to eat. Then Capt. Lewis gave more gifts. He paid particular attention to the two lesser chiefs. Then he turned to trading, giving some $30 in goods for more horses. He also gave trade items to Charbonneau and told him to get a horse for Sacagawea, for she has a great longing to see the ocean and will be coming west with us.

Toward Lemhi Pass
Aug. 24, '05

Our caravan set out midday from Camp Fortunate. We have nine horses and a mule carrying our goods. But most of the load is carried on the backs of Shoshone women.

Toward Lemhi Pass
Aug. 25, '05

We stopped at noon to cook our meat. While we ate, Charbonneau said something to Capt. Lewis, and the Captain exploded in anger. I ran over to see if I could help. I learned that before we set off this morning, Sacagawea told Charbonneau that our Captains only partly understand Cameahwait's plan. A band of Salish Indians, who are friendly with the Shoshone, are heading toward us along the pass. When they reach us, Cameahwait's people will turn around and travel east with them to the buffalo hunting grounds, leaving us stranded with no way to carry our gear.

Capt. Lewis quickly summoned Cameahwait and the two lesser chiefs for a council. Through Drewyer, he asked if what he had heard was true.

"Yes," Cameahwait said. "I must care for my people. We must go to the buffalo hunting ground before it is too late, before other bands hunt all the buffalo they need and scare the rest away. My people must have meat soon, or they will die."

Capt. Lewis nodded. He knows this is true. "I must care for my men, too," he said. "You promised to help us over the pass, Cameahwait. If you had not promised, we would not have started on this journey. I ask you to keep your promise."

Cameahwait frowned. Now the two lesser chiefs spoke up. They seemed to be saying that the Shoshone should keep their word. At last Cameahwait said that his people will take us over the pass. The extra gifts given to those two chiefs are well rewarded.

Our hunters brought in only one deer this evening. Capt. Lewis ordered them to give the whole of it to the Shoshone.

Shoshone village, Lemhi River
Aug. 27, '05

Capt. Lewis met with Cameahwait. He asked him to sell us twenty more horses. The chief agreed to try to find that number, but stopped short of promising.

Tonight Saint Peter played his fiddle. We men danced some sets and reels for the Shoshone, who appeared to enjoy the entertainment. All of us men are in good health and good spirits.

Cameahwait's people agreed to sell us the horses. But the price is sky high. Capt. Lewis tried to barter, but the Shoshone held firm. In the end the Captain paid what was asked. We now own a herd of Shoshone horses.

Before he left us, Cameahwait brought over an old, wrinkled Shoshone man. His name sounds close to Old Toby, so this is what the Captains call him.

Through Drewyer, Cameahwait said, "This man has crossed the Shining Mountains."

"Many times?" asked Capt. Lewis.

"Once," said Cameahwait. "Ten years ago."

"Ten years is a long time," said the Captain.

"Not to a mountain," said the chief. "This man can lead you through the Shining Mountains along the Nez Percé trail."

The Captains seemed unsure whether to accept this offer, but in the end, they did, for they have no other.

We told the Shoshone good-bye. They turned east, toward the buffalo. We will head west, led by Old Toby.

Made 12 miles. Capt. Lewis is sputtering about "Shoshone sharp dealers." He and Capt. Clark have now examined our new horses. Most are old and lame.

***

North of Lemhi Pass
Sept. 2, '05

Hard going. Made only $7^1/_2$ miles. There was no trail, so we had to hack through the brush. The way was steep. Several horses slipped and fell. Two died. I am very hungry.

Lost Trail Pass
Sept. 3, '05

Thermometer broke. Do not know how cold it is, but it is cold.

Our hunters brought in only a few pheasants. We ate them tonight with rain, then snow, then sleet falling. We are all hungry, yet I saw Old Toby slip some of his own supper to our dog.

Capt. Clark says he has never seen such a bad stretch for a horse. I thought the worst of the trip was behind us, but this tops all.

North of Lost Trail Pass
Sept. 4, '05

Freezing. We half walked, half slid down a steep, slippery hill to a Salish campsite. There are some four hundred in their party with some five hundred horses. The Salish wear long shirts belted at the waist. They were generous, sharing their small supply of roots and berries with us. When our hunter came in with a deer, it was our turn to share with the Salish.

North of Lost Trail Pass
Sept. 6, '05

The Captains traded some of our ailing horses plus trade goods for healthy Salish horses. We repacked our gear and made 10 miles. We had no game, so supped on Capt. Lewis's portable soup. It tasted muddy, just as Charlie and I thought back in Wood River. Still, I eagerly ate my portion.

Travelers' Rest
Sept. 9, '05

Hard going, up and down steep hills. Stopped to rest beside a stream. Capt. Lewis has named our camp accordingly.

The mountains ahead look awful.

Valley
Sept. 10, '05

A fright today. Colter and I went hunting. We shot 4 deer, 1 beaver, and 3 pheasants. We were bringing the meat back to camp when three braves appeared suddenly before us. I had not heard a sound. The three had arrows fitted in their bows. Arrows aimed at us. Colter quickly put down his gun. I did the same. We stood staring at the braves. They did not seem to want our meat. If they had, they would have taken it. Moving slowly so as not to startle them, I signed what I hoped meant for them to follow us back to camp. They agreed. We picked up our guns and led the way.

I took the braves to Drewyer. He signed with them. He cannot say what nation they are from but learned that they are chasing some Shoshone braves who stole their horses. Remembering how the Shoshone greeted us, Capt. Lewis asked Colter and me to tie bits of ribbon into the braves' hair. We did, and it seemed to please them. I also gave them some fishhooks.

Good news! Capt. Lewis has talked one of the braves into traveling with us. He will lead us west to his people, on the other side of the mountains. This brave says the trip will take five sleeps. That means six days. We of the Corps can endure any hardship for six days.

Rocky Mountains
Sept. 11, '05

Two of our horses strayed. Spent much of the day searching for them. The brave who said he would lead us to his people grew tired of waiting and left us. Immense snow-capped mountains to our left. Made 7 miles.

Hot Springs
Sept. 13, '05

Passed a hot spring with steaming water bubbling up

from the ground and spurting from the rocks into a pool. Collins and I thought to soak our freezing feet in the spring but the water was too hot.

Killed Colt Creek
Sept. 14, '05

The worst stretch yet! We were pelted with rain and hail, then nearly blinded by snow as we inched our way along. The path narrowed until it was hardly wider than a human foot. At one steep spot, I stumbled on a rock, lost my footing, and pitched headfirst down the mountain. I slid on my stomach, arms flailing, and somehow managed to grab on to a tree, which stopped me from plunging to my death. Colter put himself at risk by sliding down to me and helping me back to the path.

How glad I was when we reached a creek and made camp. Indians must have been here before us, as all the grass is nibbled away with none left for our horses. There is no game here. We are all worn down and badly in need of meat. There was nothing to do but kill one of the colts. No one enjoyed this night's supper.

Awful news. Old Toby has led us astray. No one in our party blames him. He is doing his best, but now we must retrace all those hard, cold steps. I have a bad feeling in my gut. For the first time, I wonder: Will we make it?

* * *

Up a steep and dangerous ridge. I walked behind the horse carrying Sacagawea and Pomp. Several times this horse stumbled and nearly fell. Midday, I heard an awful crash and saw the horse carrying Capt. Clark's writing desk plunging down the mountainside. The poor beast rolled until it hit a tree, smashing the desk to bits. I handed the bridle of my horse to Colter and ran down the hill after the horse. I was sure he had broke his neck, but he struggled to his feet, unhurt, only shaken. Three other horses were not so lucky this day. This is a most terrible place.

At last we reached the top of the ridge and made camp. We have no water, so boiled snow to make our soup. As I ate, I felt sick to look around and see enormous, high white peaks looming above us in every direction. O woeful sight. How will we ever get through them?

Most awful day! Woke to find myself buried under a blanket of heavy, wet snow. All of us are soaked to the bone and so cold. We set off. Every time I brushed against a pine tree it dropped wet snow onto my head. Or down my neck. I trudged ankle deep through freezing slush. My feet are froze. I cannot stop shaking. All are miserable.

Rocky Mountains
Sept. 17, '05

Our horses are near starving. They stray, looking for some-thing to eat. It took us until 1:00 today to round them up.

We stumble on through the deep snow. Old Toby keeps us on the trail by looking for scars on trees made by Nez Percé packhorses scraping their burdens against the bark.

Another colt for supper tonight. We are all half frozen. Colter's face is blue with the cold. Sacagawea keeps Pomp next to her skin for warmth. The way is too long for us to turn back. Yet we cannot go on like this much longer.

Rocky Mountains
Sept. 18, '05

The Captains have made a plan for our survival. At dawn, Capt. Clark set off with Reuben Fields and five others. This party will go ahead, hunting. If successful, they will leave game for us on the trail. If they shoot none, Capt. Lewis says we will have no choice but to begin eating our packhorses.

Rocky Mountains
Sept. 19, '05

Marched 6 miles this morning, cold and suffering. I was as downhearted as I have ever been. Old Toby clam-bered up to the top of a ridge ahead of us. He called out for us to come and look. We struggled forward and O, most wonderful sight. Green prairie! The end of these cursed mountains! Old Toby says we may reach the prairie tomorrow. It will be not a minute too soon.

Rocky Mountains
Sept. 20, '05

Hard, hard going. Two horses fell and died.

We did not reach the prairie.

We ate most of a strayed horse Capt. Clark found starving in the mountains and left hanging in a tree for us. He left a letter with the horse, telling us he is going ahead to look for the Nez Percé Indians.

Capt. Lewis wrote in his journal for hours tonight. I thought he was writing of our hardships, but when he asked me to make a copy, I discovered he had written long passages describing woodpeckers, thrushes, jaybirds, ruffled grouse, and blue grouse, including the measurements of each. I worry for his mind.

Rocky Mountains
Sept. 21, '05

Capt. Lewis's horse strayed. It is packed with all the Captain's winter woolens, so he is most eager to find it. He sent Colter and me after it, and we found the horse grazing on a small patch of green. It was mighty hard to pull that poor thin animal from the first food it had eaten in many a day, but we did so. We led the horse back to our camp in a valley, and I was so glad to see grass peeking through the snow, grass enough for all the horses.

The horses are fed now, but we men are starving. I am weak, so weak. Our supper this night was a mix of portable soup, horsemeat, crayfish, wolf, and a crow, shot by Joseph Fields. A most desperate meal.

Nez Percé village
Sept. 22, '05

We have crossed the Rocky Mountains! For eleven wretched days, we men followed our Captains. We trudged 160 miles in freezing cold, enduring extreme hunger. We were low in spirits, but no man sank to the ground in despair. Rather, we trusted in our Captains and they brought us through. Surely this was the worst we will have to suffer. Now I look behind us and feel proud to see those immense rocky giants. The Shining Mountains did not defeat our Corps!

Here we are in Parts Unknown.

How happy we were to see Reuben Fields come to meet us on our way down from the mountains. Capt. Clark sent him to bring us dried fish, as there is little game here. He says we can make camp at a Nez Percé village at the foot of the mountains. Capt. Clark and his party are camped at a second Nez Percé village farther west. Reuben says the Nez Percé are friendly. They will offer us dried salmon and camas roots to eat.

Reuben warned us, "Go easy on those roots."

We are camped beside a small Nez Percé village. There is grass. Our horses are grazing. We are all so grateful to be here tonight, grateful to be alive.

As Reuben said they would, the Nez Percé gave us dried fish and roots for our supper. I tried to hold back on the roots. I tried to ruin my appetite by thinking back to the Indian woman, spitting into my soup. But I was so very, very hungry, I could not help but eat my fill.

Canoe Camp, Kooskooske River
Sept. 30, '05

I have never been so sick. Sick and puking. My stomach swells with gas. I double over in pain and pray for a good breaking of wind to relieve it. Camas roots have put all the men in this same sorry state. Today is the first day I feel up to holding my quill, though my hand is shaky.

Capt. Lewis is too frail to stand up. Capt. Clark is sick, too, but that never stops him. He is doctoring the rest of us with Thunder Clappers. I have refused to take any, as my bowels are stormy enough on their own. We are lucky that the Nez Percé are a peaceful people, for weak as we are, they could easily take all we have and leave us to die.

***

The Nez Percé freely gave us food for several days. Now they say we must buy it from them. We have few trade goods left. I snipped the brass buttons off my uniform coat and bought a day's supply of camas roots. I know these roots will twist my gut into knots, but there is nothing else to eat.

Most of the party are still too weak to move. Whitehouse and I felt up to going hunting, but we saw no game.

Large ponderosa pines grow here. I went with those of the party who are able to walk to cut down pines to make new canoes. We began hollowing out a tree trunk with our adzes. Many Nez Percé gathered around to watch us work. An old Nez Percé chief, Twisted Hair, showed us how to lay the tree over a long, low fire. This burns its center, making it easy to scrape out the charred wood. So simple!

Drewyer and Colter are marking our horses with Capt. Lewis's branding iron. We will lead a few horses west with us. Twisted Hair's people have promised to look after the rest of our herd until we come back this way. This morning I told old Lizzy good-bye until next spring.

Our canoes are finished. We have four large and two smaller. We are packing them up. Capt. Lewis is still too sick to stand. Capt. Clark drags himself around, seeing to the Corps.

Kooskooske River
Oct. 7, '05

What a fine thing to be in a canoe traveling *down* a river! How easy to travel with the current instead of fighting against it.

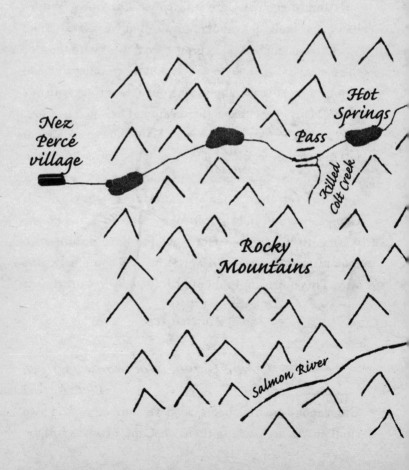

We left the Nez Percé village this afternoon and made 20 miles on the Kooskooske River, which flows into the Lewis River, so named by Capt. Clark, which flows into the Columbia. Or so Twisted Hair says. He has volunteered to come with us. He can speak to the western Indians. He says their languages are close to his own tongue.

Travelers' Rest

Rocky Mountain Dividing Ridge

Missouri River

met Salish

Headwaters of Missouri River

Wisdom River

Gallatin River

Jefferson River

Madison River

Camp Fortunate

Shoshone villages

Lemhi Pass

Lemhi River

We had to run more than a dozen rapids this day. Our canoes are not steady. Several overturned in the swift water. No one was hurt, but we lost considerable goods and wet our blankets. Still, I would not trade this for paddling up the Missouri.

Old Toby was badly scared by his rides down the rapids. Tonight when we pulled ashore, he ran away from our party. Capt. Clark saw him go. He ordered Colter to jump on a horse and go after him, as he left without his pay.

Through Drewyer, Twisted Hair told the Captains, "Let him go. The Nez Percé would only rob him of his pay when he passes through their villages."

Old Toby took two of our horses with him. I guess they will count as his pay.

Lewis River
Oct. 10, '05

What a surprise to find so many people living here in Parts Unknown! There are villages and fishing camps all along this river. Each day many Indians paddle out to greet us. Their foreheads are flat, sloping from the top of their noses to the top of their heads. Twisted Hair told us that they strap boards on the heads of their babies so as to flatten their skulls in a way they find attractive. He says they are all part of the great Nez Percé nation. Capt.

Lewis got all worked up at seeing their light, well-made canoes. They make ours seem crude and heavy.

Some days Twisted Hair and one of his men go ahead of us in a small canoe to let the native peoples know that we come in peace. Other days, Twisted Hair sticks with us, trusting that when the Indians see him traveling with us, as well as a mother and baby, they will know we are not a war party. Sacagawea is now helping our party simply by being with us.

The native people along this stretch eat dog. Some of our party are so hungry that they buy them. Capt. Clark refuses to eat dog, and so do I.

Each night we light a campfire. Indians who live close by come and sit around it with us. They all enjoy Saint Peter's fiddling and our dancing.

Lewis River
Oct. 15, '05

We paddle through great canyons here. Today we reached a stretch where the river narrowed and the water foamed and roared. Reasonable men would have taken the canoes out of the water and carried them around these rapids, however long it took. But the Corps of Discovery is no longer made up of reasonable men. With Capt. Lewis in the lead, we raced down these boiling rapids. I paddled with Whitehouse and we flew over the white spray. Drewyer's canoe was in front of ours. He hit a rock and got tossed into the

water but managed to keep hold of his boat. We lost
some bedding and clothes, but no men.

Columbia River
Oct. 16, '05

We have reached the Columbia River and are
camped on its beautiful bank. Capt. Lewis and a party
have gone ahead to explore. The water here is clear
and deep and filled with salmon. Goodrich offered to
catch some for our supper, but Twisted Hair said at
this time of year the salmon have laid their eggs and
are dying, so are not fit to eat.

Collins is gathering roots on shore as we go. What he
has in mind for them, he will not say.

Some two hundred Indians came to our campfire
tonight. They sang and danced for us quite spectacular.

Columbia River
Oct. 20, '05

We saw Indians on shore dressed in sailors' jackets. They
must have traded for them with sailors anchored off the
coast. Can we be close to the Pacific Ocean?

Capt. Lewis has returned from exploring. He looks
worried. Tonight when the campfire had burned down
and most men were asleep, he said, "We have rough

rapids and waterfalls ahead of us, Pup. I do not know how we can get through them."

Columbia River
Oct. 21, '05

Bad rapids today. Nearly swamped our canoe. Game is scarce here, so we are fish eaters now. Most of us like fish well enough, but their oily scent has attracted fleas. These little pests are worse than mosquitoes. They gnaw on every part of me.

Collins has brewed beer from those roots. I tasted it and thought it bitter, but Colter says it is outstanding.

Columbia River
Oct. 22, '05

We have reached the beginning of the most terrible rapids. The Captains and some men have gone ahead, one party on each side of the river, to see how best to get around them.

The Captains are back. They say only the first stretch of the falls must be portaged. This is a roaring 20 foot drop. The rest, they say, can be run by the Corps.

Capt. Lewis has traded items for an Indian pine canoe. It is very light, made to run swift rapids. A carving of a hawk decorates the bow. Capt. Lewis is as pleased with this craft as if he had designed it himself.

Columbia River
Oct. 23, '05

Terrible portage. We tied our elk-skin ropes to our canoes. One at a time, we lowered the canoes down a steep cliff to the river below. They were dead heavy. The ropes made deep cuts into my hands. As we lowered the last canoe, the rope Shields was holding snapped. My rope jerked out of my hands and the canoe crashed to the bottom of the falls. I was glad to see some helpful Indians jump into the river and get it.

With the boats waiting below, we loaded our gear on our backs and marched around the falls. The fleas began to bite me very bad. I looked up and saw other men wriggling and slapping at themselves. Seaman was frantic, nipping at his skin. The fleas were eating us alive. When we could bear it no longer, we flung off our packs, stripped off our clothes, and beat those fleas away. That done, we dressed again, shouldered our packs, and marched down the steep hill. When we reached the bottom of the falls, we found we had to buy our canoe back from the Indians.

Bad news from Twisted Hair. He says that the Nez Percé are at war with the Chinooks, who live below these falls. He has heard from his people to the south that the Chinooks are waiting for us eagerly. They plan to slay us and take our goods.

The Captains called us together. They ordered us to oil our rifles and check that our powder is dry. We are to load up our guns. I have one hundred rounds of ammunition, as does every man in the Corps. If the Chinooks attack us, we will be ready.

Columbia River
Oct. 24, '05

Twisted Hair left our party this morning. He did not wish to meet his Chinook enemies. Before he left, he warned us that very soon we will come to another dangerous stretch of waterfalls called the Dalles.

We have reached the Dalles. I walked with Capt. Lewis, Seaman, and others to view these falls. The water is all white foam and spray that boils and churns most terrible. I stared in silence, thinking that if we try to run these rapids, we will be lucky to come out alive. Yet the banks are too steep for a portage. What else can we do but run them?

The Captains have hired local Indians with packhorses to carry our heavy goods around the rapids. Gibson and the others who cannot swim will walk with them, leading our horses. They will carry the Captains' journals, the rifles, powder, ammunition, and Capt.

Lewis's measuring instruments. Sacagawea, Pomp, and Seaman will go with the walkers.

I was checking our canoe for cracks when I noticed a few Indians on shore. When I finished inspecting the canoe, I looked up to see throngs of Indians gathered beside the river.

Colter came over to me, grinning. "They have come to see us smash up and drown," he said cheerily, with a nod toward the spectators. "Then they plan to run into the river and grab all our goods." He rubbed his hands together in glee. "I don't plan on dying, no, sir. I plan to jump in the canoe and show those no-good scavengers how woodsmen run rapids!"

He is the only one of us looking forward to this run.

I will send this journal with Gibson. If I do not make it, I hope it will get sent home to Ma. Here we go.

We climbed into our canoes and set off into the flying spray. I paddled bow. Collins and McNeal knelt in the middle. Colter paddled stern. I was blinded by the raging water but dug my paddle into the foam, trusting that Colter could see to steer us. We jolted and bumped over the rapids. In spite of the danger, it was a thrill to be spun sideways in the falls, only to be whirled forward and slammed down by the next jolt.

At last we hit the bottom of the falls and slowed down. Only then did Colter call out that he had been completely blinded by the spray. This is none too comforting, for ahead of us, the Captains say, is a far worse stretch.

So far, we are all alive.

Here we go again, running white, foaming rapids.
There must be a thousand Indians on shore. Some of
our own men are there as well. They have ropes to
throw to us should we spill from our canoes. I only hope
our luck will hold.

The cruel rapids are behind us now. Every man survived. Two of our canoes swamped and filled with
water, but wet gear is nothing to us now.

We are camped on a high rocky ledge. Capt. Clark
calls it Fort Rock Camp, as the rocks form a natural bar-
rier. The Captains say we will stay here to dry our goods,
mend our canoes, and hunt. We are in Chinook territory. We are on our guard.

Tonight Drewyer brought in a deer and a goose. We
enjoyed a fine supper.

Our leather clothes are grimy and most attractive to
fleas. The little pests chew on us without mercy. We
solve this problem by going naked as much as possible,
as the fleas stay in our clothes.

I was standing guard this evening when I spied five Chinook canoes coming toward us. Capt. Lewis had us men keep our rifles ready as the Indians came into our fort. When all seemed peaceful, the Captains gave out medals and handkerchiefs. Our hunters had brought in five deer, and Goodrich had gigged a large trout, so we invited these Chinooks to share our meal. After supper, Drewyer tried his hand signs, but the Chinooks did not understand, so we learned nothing from them. They left soon after eating.

Colter's bobcat hat is missing. Colter is storming around, threatening to do whatever it takes to get it back.

Fort Rock Camp
Oct. 28, '05

Rainy and cold. The Chinooks visit us on a regular basis. They freely help themselves to whatever items they want. They don't see this as stealing and seem surprised when some in the Corps get angry. They have not taken anything of great value, but their thieving never lets up.

Fort Rock Camp
Oct. 29, '05

Rain all day. Whitehouse, Collins, and I went to a Chinook village to trade goods for fish. We cannot talk or sign with these people, but we came to an understanding.

After our trade, a chief invited us into his lodge. He wore a large medicine-bundle pouch around his neck. Collins pointed to it curiously. The chief opened the pouch and emptied out some dozen shriveled items. I took them to be some sort of wild mushrooms. Then I saw that each was tipped with a dried-up fingernail. We left his lodge soon after and walked quickly back to our fort.

Columbia River
Oct. 31, '05

We have left Fort Rock and are heading downriver again.

Colter's spirits are low. He never recovered his bobcat hat.

Falls of the Columbia River
Nov. 1, '05

Early fog. A stretch ahead is a great waterfall studded with large rocks, very dangerous. We are packing our gear for another portage.

My shoulder is strained from carrying the canoes $2^1/_2$ miles over the rocks. The only way we could move the big canoes was to shove them along sets of poles laid out from rock to rock. One canoe was damaged. All have small leaks from being dragged.

***

Columbia River
Nov. 2, '05

Capt. Clark says we are near the coast, and if the fog ever lifts, we may see the ocean.

The Chinooks here do a fine business with trading ships. They are rich from selling sea-otter pelts, and drive hard bargains for their wares. Capt. Lewis grumbles that we are only "hungry explorers," but the prices stay the same.

Made 29 miles today.

Columbia River
Nov. 4, '05

I went out early to hunt and got a buck.

When we stopped to make camp, we were visited by a band of Chinooks. Some were wrapped in colorful blankets. Some were dressed in sailor shirts and hats. All carried weapons: spears, bows, axes, pistols, or muskets. I kept my rifle handy. We cannot speak with these people, but the Captains smoked with them and tried to show friendship. As the Indians were leaving, Capt. Clark discovered that the very peace pipe we had just smoked was missing. He ordered a search of the Indians. Nothing was found. Then Drewyer said that his blanket cape was gone. There was another search and the cape was found stuck under some tree roots. The pipe was never found. The Captains sent the Chinooks away. We have doubled our guard.

Geese honking all last night kept us awake. Tonight we cooked up a fine supper out of those honkers. Rocky ground makes for hard sleeping. We are all cold and damp. My spirits are low.

Colter's spirits are improved. He sat down at our campfire tonight wrapped in a fine red-and-blue Chinook blanket. He will not say how he got it. He only smiles and looks contented for the first time since his hat went missing.

Capt. Lewis is bursting with excitement. He met a Chinook chief today and believes the chief was trying to tell him of a white trader who lives alone near the mouth of the Columbia River. This trader, the Captain says, must be supplied by ships that anchor off the coast. It is now the Captain's most burning desire to find this trader. He wishes to present him with President Jefferson's letter of credit so he can buy winter supplies. If a ship comes, Capt. Lewis plans to buy passage for his journals, the Scientific Notebooks, and other items and sail them back east to the President.

***

Columbia River

Thick fog this morning. I could hardly see to move around camp. As we worked, Capt. Lewis said, "Listen. Breakers!" I held my breath and at last I heard the sound of water slapping against the shore. We climbed up onto the rocky cliffs and looked westward. Fog hid the ocean from us, yet we could hear it. This has buoyed us up no end, and we danced and whooped in celebration. Rain comes down heavy, but nothing can dampen our spirits when we are this close to our goal. Most of us have never seen an ocean.

Columbia River

Nov. 8, '05

The river here is near 7 miles wide. The water is salty, not fit to drink. The waves and swells are so high that as we went today, I felt sick to my stomach. Can these river waves be the breakers that we heard? We cannot find a place to camp, the banks being too steep. The rain comes down in buckets and the fleas plague us no end.

Columbia River

Nov. 9, '05

O such a storm. Terrible! Huge trees whipped by the wind nearly swept us into the river as we huddled on the shore. One canoe went down, fully loaded with gear. We are thankful no men were aboard. Seeing that one sink, we waded out into the raging storm, unloaded the others, and dragged them onto the shore.

I put out several pots and kettles to collect rainwater, as we badly need drinking water.

The rain has let up. We are all wet to the skin. Yet thinking of the ocean ahead keeps us cheerful.

Columbia River
Nov. 10, '05

Rained so hard we could not cook or eat or even pack up our gear. Our camp is flooded. Hemmed in by a cliff, as we were, all we could do was stand in one spot while the water rose up to our knees. At last the rain stopped. We quickly loaded our canoes and set out. We paddled for 2 miles, but the swells were so big they nearly swamped us. There was no bank, only cliffs, so we could not pull over. All we could do was turn around and come back to this flooded camp.

In this same weather, five Chinooks paddled to our camp, selling fish. Their canoe skimmed over the high waves as if they were nothing.

Hungry Harbor
Nov. 12, '05

Thundered all last night, with hail and violent winds.

The fog surrounds us. I can barely see this journal page. We cannot leave our camp. The Captains had us fill our canoes with stones and sink them in the river. This was the only way they could think to keep them from being smashed by the waves.

The Captains say we are close to the ocean. Yet we cannot get there. The rain goes on and on. It is hard to bear. All these days we have been wet. We sleep in wet bedding on the wet ground. All our clothes are rotting, even the beautiful buffalo robes.

I have never felt so desperate. We are crowded together on a point of land too small to hold us all, but in this rocky terrain, it is the best we can do. The waves pound and pound at our camp. Capt. Clark has named this camp Hungry Harbor.

Columbia River Bay
Nov. 13, '05

Only a drizzle this morning. The Captains sent Colter, Willard, and me out in the Indian canoe to search for a better campsite. As we paddled off, Capt. Lewis shouted after us, "Keep an eye out for the white trader!"

We headed west, toward the mouth of the river. High swells nearly turned us over several times. At last I spied a bay. We paddled into it, found a sandy stretch of beach, and pulled ashore. The wind is not so strong here. Behind us are woods where we might hunt for game. It seems a fine site for a camp. Colter has taken the canoe and gone back to tell the main party this good news.

After Colter left, Willard and I set off to hunt. We came across five Chinooks, also hunting. They are young, no more than 15 or 16. They pointed, as if to say they come from a nearby village. We began hunting with these boys, and I shot a deer. Willard and I are now camped with them on this rainy night.

Columbia River Bay
Nov. 14, '05

Willard and I hunted with those five Chinooks. We roasted the deer I shot over our campfire and ate together. We could not speak with these boys, but Willard and I understood our sharing a meal to be a bond of trust between us. Now I know this is not the understanding they had, for when Willard and I awoke at dawn, we found our rifles missing.

The boys were gone, too. Willard and I followed their tracks and caught up to them as they were stalking a deer. Using hand signals, we told them they must return our rifles. They pretended not to understand. We shook our fists. We made every sort of sign to say that if they did not give back our guns, they would pay a heavy price. Still they held our guns.

I ran out of patience. I signed that others of our party would be here any minute and would shoot them. Not a minute later I heard a rustling noise ahead of us, and out of the brush came Capt. Lewis, Drewyer, and three more of our party. The boys stared at the men. I was as amazed as they were but lost no time in grabbing back my gun. Willard did the same. I signaled to the boys that they must lay down their bows and arrows, and they did so. By the time Capt. Lewis and his party reached us, we had the situation under control.

Capt. Lewis had seen the boys handing us our guns. Hard as it was, I had to tell him how they came to be stolen. Hearing this, the Captain's temper rose. He fumed and ranted at these boys, saying he was sick and tired of all the thieving. He made signs that clearly said if any of their people ever stole from us again, they would be shot. The Chinooks seemed to understand.

Capt. Lewis said that Willard and I must tie their hands and march these boys back to our beach camp. "Hold them as prisoners until I get there," he said.

I said, "But Captain, they are only pups."

"Pups?" Capt. Lewis said, sounding surprised. He eyed me for a moment, then looked back at the boys. "So they are," he said. "So they are." He motioned to them to pick up their bows and arrows and go back to their people, and they quickly disappeared into the trees.

Beach Camp
Nov. 17, '05

We are camped at the beach now, sheltered by the bay. Yesterday Collins and I found an abandoned Indian village in the woods. We are taking boards from the

Indian huts, soaking them to drown the colonies of fleas living inside, then toting them back to our camp to use in building our own shelters. Our hunters are bringing in as much game as we can eat. My only complaint is this: Where is the Pacific Ocean?

Beach Camp
Nov. 18, '05

Capt. Clark made a party of all those who had never seen an ocean. It included York and all us men who signed on to the Expedition in Kentucky. Charbonneau, Sacagawea, and Pomp came, too. As did Seaman, although he spent his early years at sea. We set out from our camp to walk to the coast.

On our way, we stopped by a tree. Capt. Clark showed us where Capt. Lewis had carved his name into the trunk. I took out my knife to add my name, as did all the men. I felt so proud to carve PVT. GEORGE SHANNON.

Capt. Clark finished it off by carving: BY LAND FROM THE U. STATES IN 1804 & 1805.

As we walked, a gray mist began to settle around us. Capt. Clark led us to the edge of a rocky westward-facing ledge, where he had hoped we might stand to see the ocean. All we could see was thick fog in front of us like a great gray wall. I heard the roar of breakers crashing against the rocks, I smelled salt in the air, but through that fog I could see nothing.

We stood there for some time, waiting. At last Capt.

Clark called that we must get back to camp. As we turned to go, the wind picked up and Colter yelled, "Hold up! The fog is lifting!"

I squinted toward the west. I hardly dared breathe as the fog thinned away, the sun shone through, and we were treated to such a vast and wonderful sight. The Pacific Ocean!

Sacagawea held up her son so that he might see it for himself.

How magnificent were those blue waters, stretching wide before us until far in the distance they met up with the sky. This was the spot we had paddled and marched and hacked and fought so long and so hard to

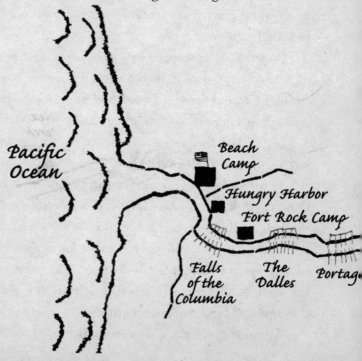

reach, and now I was there.

As we took it all in, clouds skittered over the sun and the mist gathered once more. Gray fog blew in. The ocean faded from our view.

No one spoke as we walked back to camp. I could not have said a word, I was so filled with feeling.

When we arrived at our camp, I spotted Capt. Lewis talking with a group of Chinook chiefs. He turned and waved me over. When I reached him, he gave me a slap on the back. "Now you have seen the ocean!" he said. "Was it worth the trip, Shannon?"

I found my voice. "Yes, sir," I said. *"Yes, sir!"*

Dearest Ma,

I have written of my days, as you asked, filling this journal to the very last page. And I believe that in crossing this great continent from Pittsburgh to the Pacific Ocean, I have come to know my heart. If some bits here are too rough for you, Ma, I am sorry, but my Captain said I must tell all as it happened, and so I have.

It has not been an easy journey. We overcame great difficulties. It is hard to say which was worse, the frozen mountain peaks, the prickly pears, or the raging herds of mosquitoes.

We have had such fine times, too, dancing round blazing fires to the beat of Mandan drums, eating roasted buffalo, sleeping out under the stars. We found no saber-tooth tigers, no 7 foot beavers, yet we saw the sky glow with wild colors of the Northern Lights and the prairie blooming and filled with every sort of bird and bounding creature. Oh, Ma, when I set off on this Adventure, I never

dreamed our land could hold so many
wonders. And to think that I was there to
see them with my own eyes. It is my hope
that in reading this journal, you and
Thomas, John, James, Nancy, Lavinia,
and the little ones may travel on my words
across this great, fine land and see it, too.

Capt. Lewis is still chasing after that
lone white trader. If he finds him, and if
a ship should come, I will send this journal home to you. If no ship comes, then I
will carry it back to you myself.

I am binding up a new journal now.
Capt. Lewis has given me the pages. I
will cover it with the hide of an elk I
shot myself. Whatever happens on the
trip back home, you can count on me to
write it down.

Soon we will move to our new winter
camp. I am in good health, and if this
rain ever lets up, I will be in good spirits,
too.

Your loving son,
George

AUTHOR'S NOTE

At family gatherings when I was young, my uncle Robert Hall used to tell my cousins and me stories of our ancestor George Shannon, who, at age sixteen, ran away from home to explore the west with Lewis and Clark. George was a great romantic figure of my youth. When I decided to write about him and began researching the Expedition, I discovered that, while some historians put his age at sixteen when he joined up with Capt. Lewis, others believe he was seventeen or eighteen. My George Shannon was sixteen when he ran off, and so he remains in my novel of the Expedition.

Young George Shannon's daily life did not merit much ink in either of the Captains' journals. What facts I learned about him, I used as the skeleton for his fictional journal and filled in the rest with what might have been. And once, what never was. When the Corps of Discovery was closing in on the source of the Missouri River, the water became so shallow that river travel was nearly impossible. On August 9, 1805, the real George Shannon was with a party of men led by Capt. Clark, straining their muscles lugging dead heavy canoes loaded with supplies up a rocky river bed and getting eaten alive by mosquitoes. Meanwhile, Capt. Lewis, Drewyer, Shields, and McNeal hiked off in search of the Shoshone, hoping to buy horses from them for a portage over the Rocky Mountains. George had already done considerable lugging, and since this journal is his story, his journey, I decided to let him trade places with McNeal so that he—and the reader—might go off with Capt. Lewis and experience firsthand one of the greatest adventures of the Expedition.

George Shannon returned to St. Louis in September 1806 with the Corps of Discovery. From there, he traveled home to Ohio, where he delighted his ma by giving her his journals of the Expedition. The following year, Chief Big White traveled to Washington to meet with President Jefferson, and George joined a party escorting him from Washington back to his village. Along the way, a band of Arikara attacked the Mandan chief, and George was shot in the leg. The leg had to be amputated, and he was fitted with a wooden one. George, nicknamed Pegleg Shannon, went on to study law and became a member of the Kentucky House of Representatives. When Missouri became a state in 1821, he moved there to practice law and was later elected to the Missouri Senate.

—K.M.

AUTHOR'S ACKNOWLEDGMENTS

Embarrassing, but true: It took me longer to research and write this book than it took the Corps of Discovery to make its way from St. Louis to the Pacific Ocean and back again. It might have taken even longer without the good help of many good people. My thanks to Grace Hall Kettenbrink for sending me her Shannon family papers, and to Cathee Adderton, Andrew Zebell, Jenny Vaughan, Marky Shapleigh, and Linda Bridges for outstanding service as St. Louis media escorts and ace research associates.

I would also like to thank my corps: Jim McMullan, Leigh McMullan, Judy Sweets, Ron Ukrainetz, Lynette Scriver, everyone at the Lewis and Clark Trail Heritage Foundation in Great Falls, Holly McGhee, Adrienne Yorinks, Joanna Cotler, Alicia Mikles, and especially Justin Chanda, my incredible editor.

Adrienne Yorinks has illustrated several books for children. Her textile art appears in many private and public collections throughout the United States and around the world. One of her commissions, created for the AFL-CIO, hangs in the organization's headquarters in Washington, D.C. Her most recent book, QUACK!, is a Parents' Choice Recommended book. She lives in New Jersey with her husband, two stepchildren, and two red poodles.